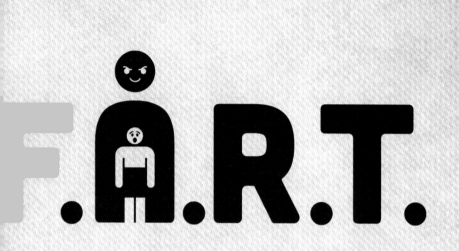

F.A.R.T.

THE F.A.R.T. DIARIES

TOP SECRET! NO KIDS ALLOWED!

PETER BAKALIAN

ALADDIN

NEW YORK   LONDON   TORONTO   SYDNEY   NEW DELHI

Book No. 1

ALADDIN

An imprint of Simon & Schuster Children's Publishing Division

1230 Avenue of the Americas, New York, New York 10020

First Aladdin hardcover edition May 2022

Text copyright © 2022 by Peter Bakalian

Cover illustration, illustration of popcorn icon throughout, and illustrations on pages 6, 13–14, 16 (bottom), 23–24, 38 (logo), 42, 53, 58, 61, 65 (dollar bill in envelope), 71, 74, 80, 85, 95 (bottom), 98, 124 (logo), 131, and 132 copyright © 2022 by Luke Lucas

Illustrations of textured paper and graph paper throughout by iStock

Illustrations on pages 9, 16 (top), 21, 37, 39, 64, 72, 81, 90, 92, 95 (top), 100–102, 106, 111–112, and 133–134 by iStock

Photographs on pages 2, 17, 22, 28, 35, 37–38, 44, 52, 60, 65, 67, 72, 75, 96, 101, 106–108, 111–112, 117–119, 124, 126, 128, 130, and 132–134 by iStock

Insert photographs and illustrations on pages 2–23 by iStock

All rights reserved, including the right of reproduction in whole or in part in any form.

ALADDIN and related logo are registered trademarks of Simon & Schuster, Inc.

For information about special discounts for bulk purchases, please contact Simon & Schuster Special Sales at 1-866-506-1949 or business@simonandschuster.com.

The Simon & Schuster Speakers Bureau can bring authors to your live event. For more information or to book an event contact the Simon & Schuster Speakers Bureau at 1-866-248-3049 or visit our website at www.simonspeakers.com.

Cover designed by Heather Palisi

Interior designed and additional illustrations provided by Heather Palisi and Ginny Kemmerer

Visual concept conceived by Peter Bakalian

The illustrations for this book were rendered digitally.

The text of this book was set in Serifa.

Manufactured in China 0122 SCP

2 4 6 8 10 9 7 5 3 1

Library of Congress Control Number 2021944669

ISBN 9781534436190 (hc)

ISBN 9781534436206 (ebook)

For Richard

DIARY 1
RIDE AT YOUR OWN RISK

The guys who run amusement parks won't tell you this, but all the really good rides have a secret exit just before you get on them. It's true. They call it a "Chicken Hatch," and it's for people who lose their nerve at the last minute.

Me, I think it's wrong to call people "chicken" because they don't want to vompedo their lunch on some roller coaster. That's why I'm offering you a chance to exit this diary right now.

I'm serious. I've kept this journal in case something should happen to me, but the detours and trapdoors that follow could easily scramble your eggs. But before you leave, consider this: **F.A.R.T. wants you to take this exit.**

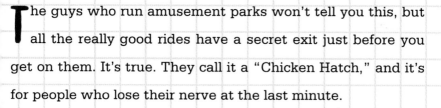

Yes, you heard that right—**F.A.R.T.** They want you to laugh at their ridiculous name and go back to eating your cornflakes because you're not supposed to know anything about them. Not you or your friends or any kids anywhere.

Now, if you're still with me, ask yourself this question:

ARE YOUR PARENTS SUDDENLY SMARTER?

I mean a *lot* smarter. Do they always find your hiding places for junk food, like the Pringles can you disguised as a fire extinguisher or the cake frosting you use for toothpaste? Have they recently discovered that you've rigged the thermometer in the medicine chest to read *10,000 degrees* when you want a sick day, or put Meow Mix on your veggies so your cat will eat them?

How about you? Has a change come over you at school? Do you high-five your teacher when she pulls a pop quiz, remind substitute teachers that homework is due, or tell fellow students, *You only hurt yourself when you forge a bathroom pass*? Sound familiar?

And riddle yourself this: When your parents go to a PTO meeting, where do they really go? IS there a PTO? Have *you* ever been to a meeting? Of course not.

Like you, I ignored these warning signs until I stumbled onto the truth. It was a bizarre truth that made sense of it all, but none of my so-called friends could believe it. If you must know, they laughed at me. The fools!

What I needed were people who could grasp the incredible. People I could trust. And I needed them now.

That was when I called **THE ONLY ONLYS**.

DIARY 2
THE ONLY ONLYS

I had never used a pay phone before, and it took me forever to find one, but I couldn't trust my cell anymore. Nor should you. After I dialed the number, **CRABAPPLE** (not her real name, though it should be) answered on the first ring.

"Speak."

"It's **POPCORN**," I said.

"It is? What number are you calling from?"

"That's not important. I need a meeting with the Only Onlys today."

I could hear her typing. She was always typing.

"No, not today," she replied.

"What do you mean *no*?"

"'No.' It's in the dictionary after 'goodbye.' Goodbye, Popcorn."

"Hold it! This is serious. *I'm* serious."

"You? Serious? I'm on a deadline for a Big Story that'll get me into Journalism Camp. That's serious. Tell you what, let me switch you to voice mail, and you can—"

"Voice mail? Who do you think you are—tech support? You're about to miss THE biggest news story of your life."

The typing stopped.

"What Big Story?"

"I'll tell you at the meeting."

"At least give me a hint."

"**F.A.R.T.**"

"Gross! When are you going to grow up? Goodbye, Popcorn, and I mean it."

"Wait! Isn't this what the Only Onlys are about—coming when one of us calls?"

"Don't tell me what the Only Onlys are about!" she snapped. "I came up with the name."

"Then come up with a meeting place. Someplace secret. Like one of those empty houses that your mom is selling. This is your last chance."

The line went quiet for what seemed like two years. Had

I gone too far with that "Big Story" stuff? Had she hung up? Was I being watched? *Do all pay phones smell like feet?*

She came back with an address and told me to use the rear entrance.

"Can the other Only Onlys make it?" I asked.

"**APRICOT** adores you, and **BANANA** (also not their real names) has no life. They'll be there. Popcorn, this had better be good."

"It isn't."

"Excellent," she said, and hung up.

I guess good reporters love bad news.

I skateboarded down dead-end streets and dark alleys to make sure I wasn't followed. When I got to Crabapple's meeting place, I found a run-down store for rent with an old sign tacked on to the back door: **SQUID KIDS PRESCHOOL**.

Yikes! No wonder the address seemed familiar. This was my old preschool, or what was left of it. I remembered my first day there: an only child dropped

into a cauldron of KIDS—all kinds of kids—criers, liars, biters, bullies, screamers, and even a kid who could pass gas to the tune of "Bananaphone"! Had he learned other songs since then? I wondered.

I opened the door slowly as if there was still a riot going on inside, but instead I saw Crabapple sitting in the same corner that had once corralled the Reading Rodeo, her favorite hangout as a child. (The rest of us slackers preferred Crayon Canyon.) Typing on her laptop and dressed in her private-school blazer, starched collar, and black tie, she looked like a person who fires other people. People like me, for example.

DIARY CODE NAME: Crabapple
Reporter at Pollywolly Prep School newspaper . . . Voted Most Likely to Disagree . . . "I don't like being right. I just am." Spelling Bee Beastmaster . . . "You don't plug it in. It's a book, dummy." Goal: Journalism Camp, change the world with THE BIG STORY.

"Of all the places to meet, why did you choose Squid Kids?" I asked.

She didn't look up. I wasn't worthy of a glance. "I forgot it was here," she said, "until I saw that stupid sign."

"Remember when Apricot painted those screaming kids on it?" I asked.

She nodded. "It was an improvement. I mean, it's not even

a squid. It's an octopus with *six* arms. Idiots." She shut her laptop so hard it must have voided its warranty, and then she aimed her lasers at me. "Okay, what's your Big Story?"

Before I could answer, a wave of peach perfume rushed up my nose.

"Popcorn!"

Apricot tackled me from behind and giggled as we fell to the floor. Imagine a Hello Kitty sundae topped with cherry hair and golden glitter. That was Apricot. It's not something I'd order at DQ, but on her it worked.

DIARY CODE NAME: Apricot
Artist, poet, attends Atomic Science Junior High (under protest) . . . *"It's all good."* . . . Can speak emoji. Personality: Creative, Disease to Please . . . Goal: Convince Crayola to bring back heliotrope-colored crayons.

The words gushed out of her as we helped each other up. "I love your View-Tube videos. Did you stop making them? Can you believe we're back at Squid Kids? Popcorn, you don't look so good. No matter. We'll fix it. Big news!" She pulled a book out of her tote bag. "I finished my book of poetry. I even worked the name 'ONLY' into the title. See?"

A glance inside the book told me that it was very Apricot—kittens, friendship, twilight, flowers, butterflies . . . you get the idea.

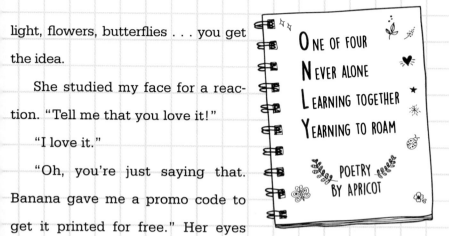

ONE OF FOUR
NEVER ALONE
LEARNING TOGETHER
YEARNING TO ROAM

POETRY
BY APRICOT

She studied my face for a reaction. "Tell me that you love it!"

"I love it."

"Oh, you're just saying that. Banana gave me a promo code to get it printed for free." Her eyes darted about the empty rental space. "Hey, where is Banana?"

CRASH!

A shock wave rattled the store's light fixtures and knocked the FOR RENT sign off the front door.

"Guess," said Crabapple.

A fast-moving electro-biker had met a slow-moving mailbox in front of the store, saved by his massive black crash helmet, the kind used by human cannonballs in the circus. He staggered around the entrance until Crabapple unlocked the door and Apricot led him to a chair. Banana was wearing the same *Supreme* shirt with the same Mountain Dew Kickstart stains from when I saw him last. This was no surprise. An ace gamer like Banana could spend weeks on end in his room blasting around the universe, which also explained why he smelled like the Moons of Endor.

Apricot tapped on his dark visor. "Can you see out of that thing?"

"No," was his muffled reply.

"Then why do you wear it?"

"Protection from gamma rays, of course." He pried off his helmet and found a half-eaten Slim Jim inside. He offered it to Crabapple, who glared her refusal.

"I know this place," he said as his eyes adjusted to the light.

"Yeah," I said, "this used to be Squid Kids."

"No, after that. My parents sent me back here when it became WonderWords and back again when it became Vowel Power."

"Oh?" said Crabapple. "Did they ever get their money back?"

"Don't listen to her," said Apricot to Banana. "We're all special in our own way. Anyway, it's Popcorn we've come to hear."

"You're right," said Crabapple as she pulled down the front window shade. "Popcorn," she commanded, "it's time for show-and-tell."

DIARY CODE NAME: Banana
White hat hacker, Comic-Con costume judge . . . "I've got an app for that." . . . 7-Eleven Customer of the Year . . . "I have a promo code for that." . . . Has a Microsoft security update named after him . . . Goals: Destroy all black hat hackers. Meet Batman.

DIARY 3
HOW I FOUND IT

It really did feel like show-and-tell. We even sat in our old assigned seats—Apricot, Banana, Crabapple, and I—four kids that you'd never see hanging together except on a derpy poster in the guidance office, you know, the kind that says **TEAMWORK IS COOL! YAY!**

It was odd that we'd still come together when one of us called. Being the only *only* children in Squid Kids had bonded us, but that was long ago. Our schools were different, and so were our friends. Maybe as only children we wanted to be the brothers and sisters we'd never had, and so we were.

"Stop stalling, Popcorn," said Crabapple, cautiously eyeing

the front door. "My mother could show up at any second with a buyer for this dump."

She was right. I was stalling, but how do you tell a nutball story without sounding like a nutball yourself?

Then Apricot came to my rescue. "Popcorn, if this was a movie, how would it begin?"

"A movie?"

"Yes, what's the first thing we'd see?"

"My house."

"When?"

"About a week ago."

"How were you feeling?"

"Happy."

"Why?"

"Because things were going great. The three kids on my payroll had shown up on time, which freed me up to shoot my ViewTube video before my parents got home."

"A payroll? What do these kids do?" asked Crabapple.

"My chores. You know—walking the dog, taking out the garbage, completing my chemistry project, mowing the lawn. The usual."

"Whoa! A chemistry project is not 'the usual,'" said

Crabapple. "You pay some kid to do your homework?"

"Not just any kid, an honor student."

"You can't do that."

"When you hire someone, you've got to pay them," I replied. "It's the law."

"He's right," agreed Banana.

"Where are you getting this money?" persisted Crabapple.

"I told you—from my ViewTube channel, Furious Popcorn's Snack Attack! I've got, like, ten thousand subs, or *had* them. That's how this whole thing started. See, while my parents were at work, I set up our kitchen to shoot an episode

where I'd secretly replace the KaleNuts Fiber Bars in my lunch with cookie dough."

"That's what your channel is about?" asked Crabapple. "Junk food?"

"I don't use that term. I believe in nutritional equality."

"It's junk."

"Okay, it's junk. Anyway, I rate the latest potato chips, explain how to hide Pop-Tarts around the house in case of emergency, test new flavors for gum companies—"

"But don't your parents run a health-food store?" asked Crabapple.

"Indeed. That's why I disguise myself with shades and a hoodie. If they ever found out, there'd be no more channel, no more payroll, and no more free swag from snack companies. And then where would I be?"

"In juvey?" said Crabapple. "Where you belong?"

"Crabapple," said Apricot, "don't interrupt the movie."

I continued: "So, to make the cookie dough, I first washed my hands. You know, I once found a Band-Aid inside an ice

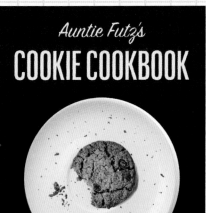

pop, so I know the value of clean food prep."

"Too much information," muttered Crabapple.

"Then, I reached for an Auntie Futz cookbook off the shelf, but when I grabbed it, I tore its cover. That's when I saw that it wasn't a cookbook at all. It was . . . well, it was . . ."

"What was it? What did you see under its cover?" asked Apricot.

"You won't believe me."

"Come on, dude, finish the movie," said Banana. "You don't get killed in the end, do you?"

"How can he get killed?" snapped Crabapple. "He's standing right there. Out with it, Popcorn!"

"It was a parenting manual," I replied.

My announcement hung in the air like a piñata.

Naturally, Crabapple took the first swing. "That's it? A parenting manual? That's the Big Story? That's why you called us together? There are millions of them out there."

"Not like this one. It's a *secret* parenting manual."

"Oh, really? Let's see it," she said.

"I don't have it with me."

"Why not?"

"Because it might explode if I remove it from my home."

"Explode. Yeah, sure. Okay, then, why didn't you take pictures of it?"

"I tried. All the shots came out fuzzy. They must have used a special paper to print the manual."

Crabapple had that tired look of a parent listening to a

child explain how a magic zebra had eaten all the cupcakes. "Can you describe this secret book that might explode?"

"I'll never forget it."

"Good. Now we're getting somewhere." She flipped open her professional reporter's notebook (it said so on the cover) and clicked a gel pen. "Start talking."

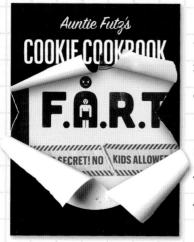

I began with the manual's cover. "'*The Number One Guide to Hacking Your Kids*,' it said. By Families Against Rotten Teens, or **F.A.R.T.** It sounded like a joke. I thought, *Were 'S.N.O.T.' and 'B.A.R.F.' already taken?* But maybe a name like '**F.A.R.T.**' was supposed to trick me into thinking it was a joke book.

"The next few pages were meant to scare off kids who found the cookbook by accident, like me."

"Popcorn," said Crabapple, "where was this book printed? Where did your parents buy it?"

"The next few pages answered some of those questions," I replied. I did my best to describe them.

HI, KIDS!

I'm Auntie Futz. Do your parents know you're reading this cookbook? Don't you know that cooking can be dangerous? Ovens explode all the time. Let your parents take those chances. They're old. And anyway, these recipes stink. So, put this book back, like, right now, or Auntie Futz will tell the tooth fairy to bring you nothing forever and ever. And I can do it too.

Love,
Auntie Futz

Are there dots blinking between the squares?

DROP THE BOOK. EXIT THE AREA.
THANK YOU.

CONGRATULATIONS, PARENTS!

YOU'RE IN!

YOU'VE MADE IT!

YOU'RE ONE OF US!

Greetings, `Mr. & Mrs. Parents`,
Do not scream or jump for joy, even though
this is the happiest day of your life. Do not
draw attention to yourselves, especially in front
of your kids.

Our records indicate that your kid(s) have
reached their "Rotten Years." You are now
ready for this manual.

`Mr. & Mrs. Parents`, did you know that
your parents and their parents all the way back to
ancient times read some version of this manual?
It's true. And now, so shall you. . . .

We are **F.A.R.T.**—Families Against Rotten Teens.
Our spies monitor rotten-kid activity everywhere
and share it with our members. Remember
PostYourPARENTSweirdUNDERWEAR.com? Well,
our parents were warned and hid their underwear. Did you?

Who are our spies?

You are! All parents are. We're all in on it! Ha-ha! Go
ahead and laugh. You've earned it.

We know all about you.

Mr. & Mrs. Parents, YOU were rotten once, just
like your kids. When YOUR parents went to a PTO
meeting, do you know where they really went? They went to
see us! (By the way, there is no PTO.)

Stop being a wimp!

All your troubles began after you taught your kids the alphabet. Back then, you believed all those books about your kids' self-esteem. Well, what about YOUR self-esteem? We saw your underwear on that website!

You're holding dynamite in your hands!

This manual will render your kids powerless, but the manual must remain secret or it won't work.

Be careful!

If your kids ever see manual number 3278, we'll repossess it, expel you, and convince everyone that your kids made the whole thing up. Sorry.

Lola Butcher

Lola Butcher, President and Loving Parent

"So, it's like our parents are in on this big joke?" asked Apricot.

"Yeah," I replied, "and we're the joke."

Crabapple looked up from her notebook. "Popcorn, all parent manuals try to control kids. What makes **F.A.R.T.** any different?"

"They don't play fair. They're organized. They share dirty tricks from one parent to another. From one generation to the next. It's like, it doesn't matter who wins, as long as kids lose. And then there's security."

Apricot clutched Banana's black helmet like a protective teddy bear. "**F.A.R.T.**'s security? Like a police force? OMG!"

"Yep."

"With uniforms and stuff?"

"You got it."

Banana whistled through his teeth. "Far out."

"Oh, come on," said Crabapple. "I've never seen them."

"You might have," I said, "but you didn't realize it."

DIARY 4
SECURITY

 hat do you mean, I 'might have' seen **F.A.R.T.**'s security?" asked Crabapple.

"Yeah, what do these goons look like?" asked Banana.

"Like plumbers," I replied, "ordinary plumbers. Except they go after leaks in **F.A.R.T.**'s secrecy."

"So, if kids don't behave, the Plumbers go after them?" asked Apricot.

"Not exactly," I replied.

I didn't want to get ahead of myself, so I described the manual's Security section and its leader, Stig Plunger—a bad guy. A very bad guy.

⛨ SECURITY

Hello, **Mr. & Mrs. Parents**.

I'm **STIG PLUNGER**, head of **F.A.R.T.**'s security team, the 24-Hour Plumbers. We're "plumbers" because we fix security leaks. The best part is—because we're dressed as plumbers, no one ever questions what we do or where we go. Sometimes we even park in handicapped spaces!

REASONS WHY WE WILL GET IN YOUR FACE:

- You discuss **F.A.R.T.** out in the open.
- You don't respond to our letters.
- You leave the manual where kids can get it.
- You fail to change the manual's cover regularly.
- You lose the manual.

SECURITY (CONTINUED)

Also, **WE CAN DESTROY YOUR MANUAL BY REMOTE CONTROL**. Cool, huh? Occasionally we'll send you a notice that includes the meter below. This is your manual's self-destruct status. **ALWAYS CHECK YOUR METER!**

Meter indicates your manual's chance of self-destruct

Remember, it's our manual, not yours. We'll blow it up if we want. **BOOM!** Just like that. Don't make us do it. Once you are cut from **F.A.R.T.**, there is no coming back.

ENJOY THE MANUAL AND HAVE A GREAT DAY!

"So, this Stig Plunger guy can destroy any manual by remote control?" asked Crabapple.

"That's why I couldn't bring it here," I replied. "If my parents reported it missing, **F.A.R.T.** could blow it up, and I'd have no proof."

"What did the rest of the manual look like?" asked Apricot.

"The last thing I saw was the table of contents. There were twelve sections."

I sketched each of the chapter titles on a whiteboard that the last renter had left behind.

"That's as far as I got in the manual. At that point my parents came home, and I had only seconds to tape up the manual's cover and put it back on the shelf. I was pretty sure I got the kitchen back to normal, not that anything would be normal again."

MANUAL SECTIONS

PRANKS SCHOOL CONTEST

HEALTH SPY TIME GAMES

EAT HOROSCOPE WORDS

HOME MONEY DA LAW

KID LIT CYBERWARE SELF-HELP

DIARY 5
WHAT WOULD YOU DO?

After my parents came home, I went to my room and waited for it to stop spinning. My mind raced. 'How could I have been so blind? My mom and dad belong to a secret gang of parents that created this insane manual, and I'm spending my time hiding Pop-Tarts in my underwear!'"

"What did you do?" asked Banana.

"I know what I'd do," said Apricot. "I would talk to them about it."

"I thought of that," I replied, "but what if they said that it *was* a joke book? They could deny the whole thing and ditch the manual before I could see it again."

"Call the police," said Banana. "Adults are always calling the cops on kids."

"And say what?" I asked. "'Officer, I'd like to a report a **F.A.R.T.**'? And what would they do? Send someone over to sniff around? And remember—a lot of cops are parents. They'd want to keep the manual a secret."

"Parents are everywhere," said Banana to himself.

I nodded. "You said it, bro."

"Do all parents have a manual?" asked Crabapple.

"I'm not sure. It may be like a special club."

"Why didn't you call us the second you found it?" asked Apricot.

"Well, I decided that this was my problem and it was my duty to solve it. I believe in taking responsibility."

"Try again, snack boy," scoffed Crabapple.

"Because I looked like an idiot, okay?"

"Much better."

"So what *did* you do?" asked Apricot.

DIARY 6
KNOW YOUR ENEMY

didn't know what to do about **F.A.R.T.**," I confessed to the Only Onlys, "because I didn't know what I was dealing with. All I knew was that THIS fool had to go to school—**F.A.R.T. SCHOOL**." I unfolded a wad of notes from my pocket and read aloud from them.

"On **DAY ONE** I started where everyone starts—I Googoled **F.A.R.T.**, its president, Lola Butcher, and its security chief, Stig Plunger. What came back was unlike anything I'd ever seen:

Googol   "F.A.R.T."

All   News   Books   Images   Videos   More

Your search "F.A.R.T." did not match any documents. Stop bothering us. Get lost.

"On **DAY TWO** I shot a special video for my ViewTube channel, Furious Popcorn's Snack Attack!, where I told my subscribers about **F.A.R.T.** and how to find a manual:

"*'The* **F.A.R.T.** *manual is probably in your home. It may be disguised as a cookbook or some old-guy book that you'd never read, like* Pickleball Is Cool! *or* Hello, Hernia. *If you find one, leave a comment below, but don't let your parents know about it. Thanks, and stay furious, my friends!'*

"I hit the upload button and waited for the video to appear on

my channel, but when I logged on to ViewTube, this is what I saw.

"Even worse, ViewTube had canceled my channel altogether. Furious Popcorn's Snack Attack! had been whacked.

"On **DAY THREE** I got a music lesson. It started when I overheard my parents say the word '**F.A.R.T.**' When I asked them what they were talking about, they froze for a few seconds, and then my dad said, 'Oh, we were discussing a rapper with one of those unusual names, called . . . Fart, uh . . .' He struggled for the next word.

"'Za-Lot,' said my mother, coming to his rescue.

"'Ubetcha,' added my dad.

"'Fart Za-Lot Ubetcha?' I asked. 'That's his name?'

"They nodded, somewhat embarrassed.

"Later, when I Googoled 'Fart Za-Lot Ubetcha,' nothing came up, but that night my inbox pinged with updated results. I clicked on the link, and this loser (below) appeared."

Apricot raised her hand as if we were still in Squid Kids. "Popcorn, you're saying that **F.A.R.T.** created a bogus website for a bogus rapper just to cover for your parents?"

"Exactly," I said. "They even created a song list of his greatest hits."

Banana was in awe. "They managed to create songs, code a new website, and get it on Googol's radar in one day? Man, they don't kid around."

FART ZA-LOT UBETCHA PLAYLIST

"I LEFT MY FART IN SAN FRANCISCO"

"DON'T PHUNK WITH MY FART"

"LISTEN TO YOUR FART"

"STOP DRAGGIN' MY FART AROUND"

"QUEEN OF FARTS"

"MADAM PAKLAVA KNOWS ALL"

"OWNER OF A LONELY FART"

"YOU'RE A FART BREAKER"

"Neither do the 24-Hour Plumbers."

"You saw them?" asked Apricot.

"Yes," I replied, "the very next day." I looked through my notes and continued. "Okay, on **DAY FOUR**, the Plumbers came to visit. I had just come home from school when I saw a van parked in our driveway. The sign on it read: **24-HOUR PLUMBERS. A GREAT PLACE TO TAKE A LEAK.** *I froze in my tracks.* **F.A.R.T.**'s secret police were in my home. My home!"

"Why were they there?" asked Apricot.

"My parents must have seen the torn cookbook cover and called them. I bet the Plumbers were searching my room to find out what else I knew. Maybe even laughing at my Boba Fett pj's! I hate these guys.

"I stayed outside and hid behind our garden gnome until the front door opened and two guys came out and hopped into the van. As they pulled out of the driveway, I followed on my skateboard, hoping they'd lead me to **F.A.R.T.**'s headquarters, but when I caught up with them, the sign on the side of this van had changed to **WOW COW ICE CREAM**. I couldn't understand it—did I chase the wrong van? How does a plumbing van disappear into thin air?"

"Maybe it was abducted by aliens whose toilets were backed up," suggested Banana.

Crabapple wrote down Banana's words and then crossed them out.

"When I got home, I asked my parents about the plumbing van, and they said something about the sewer, but I didn't believe it. Then they gave me the look that said, *We know that you know, so watch out!*

STOCK PHOTO OF PARENT GIVING THE LOOK

"What *had* the Plumbers done during their visit? Had they planted spy cams around the house to try to catch me reading the manual? Was my cell spying on me too? Why not? My parents controlled my phone plan.

"On **DAY FIVE** I got off the grid. I stopped emailing, texting, Instagramming, and FaceTiming. If **F.A.R.T.** wanted to keep track of me, I wouldn't make it easy for them. I even swept our home daily, looking for listening devices. My parents were thrilled—I was off tech and cleaning the house—the perfect son!

"And then I wondered, when my parents went out at night, where did they go? Oh, they'd say they were going to a PTO meeting or a book club, but where did they really go? Did they visit a local chapter of **F.A.R.T.**, where they traded stories on how to trick kids? Did they wear **F.A.R.T.** sweatshirts and learn secret handshakes that meant *I'm a* **F.A.R.T.** *parent and it's*

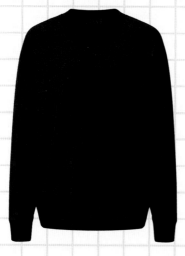

awesome? Did they learn code words so they could talk about **F.A.R.T.** right in front of me?

"When I mentioned **F.A.R.T.** at school, everyone laughed, which, of course, was the genius of **F.A.R.T.** in naming themselves '**F.A.R.T.**' It got me to thinking: Were some (or all!)

of my friends already under **F.A.R.T.**'s spell? I was surrounded by suspects—the Grade Grubbers, the Hand Raisers, the AP Kids, the Junior Hall Monitors, the Extra-Credit Fiends, the Apple Polishers, the Worriers, and even the Cheaters. And what about me? Was I falling under **F.A.R.T.**'s spell? Have you?"

I could see the Only Onlys shooting suspicious glances at each other.

"On **DAY SIX**, the nightmares came. They were always the same: I'm circling this drain, see? Actually, it's a huge toilet and I'm hanging on to the side so I don't get sucked down into the sewer where Stig Plunger and his 24-Hour Plumbers are waiting for me, but the water is like a rushing whirlpool. It's so strong that I can't hold on any longer and I start to circle . . ."

THE WORST WATER PARK IN THE WORLD!!

"Popcorn?" Crabapple whispered to me.

". . . and swirl . . ."

"Popcorn!" she repeated louder.

". . . and twirl . . ."

"POPCORN, SHUT UP!"

I was jerked back into the present by Crabapple, who had her ear to the front door.

We could hear the jangling of keys in the lock. "Hello?" a voice called out. "Is anyone in there?"

Crabapple switched off the lights. "My mom!" she hissed.

I hated this room in the dark. It reminded me of when my parents were late picking me up.

"Crabapple, do you have another place we can go?" I asked.

"There's only one place we're going," she replied, "and that's to your house. I don't care if that manual blows up in my face. I want to see it."

Apricot nodded in agreement and Banana gave me a thumbs-up.

"All right," I replied. "Follow me."

Crabapple's mom entered the store just as we escaped out the back. I was happy to have the Only Onlys by my side, but sad that they were entering my nightmare.

40

DIARY 7
IN OR OUT?

Luckily, my house was dark when we arrived. That meant my parents weren't home and I could get my hands on their **F.A.R.T.** manual disguised as a cookbook. I led the Only Onlys into the kitchen and took it off the shelf. As I handed it to Crabapple, I warned her: "What you are about to see cannot be unseen. Your life will never be the same."

"I'll take my chances," she replied flatly.

"And be careful. It's rigged to explode."

"Yeah, yeah, yeah." She waved me off as she opened the book and thumbed through the pages. "This is amazing, Popcorn," Crabapple marveled. "I've never seen anything like this—a cookbook disguised as a cookbook."

I looked over her shoulder and saw that it WAS a cookbook. Had my parents switched it? Or did the Plumbers do it?

All I could get out was, "THAT was a secret parenting manual. I know what I saw."

"You think you know what you saw," she said, "but you didn't."

"Let's face it, Popcorn," she lectured, "you have this thing about outsmarting your parents—about sneaking junk food, fooling your teachers, launching money schemes, scoring free candy, messing with honor students—"

Banana pointed at me. "You rock, dude!"

"No, he doesn't," fumed Crabapple. "The amazing Furious Popcorn is juggling so much garbage in his head that when he discovers some goofy manual, he thinks the whole world is against him. Think about it. So far we've got a cookbook that's not really a cookbook but it really is a cookbook but it's supposed to be an evil manual that controls kids—which can be blown up by remote control by a guy who has an army of secret plumbers who also sell ice cream. Oh, and as a special bonus, we get a front row seat to Popcorn's toilet-surfing dreams. My, what a Big Story this turned out to be. Thank you, Popcorn. Thanks a lot."

"Hey, not so fast," said Banana. "There *could* be a **F.A.R.T.** There's a whole secret history out there that we're not supposed to know about. Do you know that there's a Club Med on the moon for billionaires?"

"Oh, stop believing everything you read on the internet," said Crabapple.

"I don't," replied Banana.

"No? Remember that essay you wrote? The one about George Washington?"

"Sure."

"How did you say George Washington died?"

"I kinda forgot."

"You said he died on the *Titanic* when it exploded."

"History can be so sad," said Apricot.

"That's not history!" railed Crabapple. "It's people making stuff up."

43

TITANIC

"I did not make this up," I insisted.

"I'd like to say something," said Apricot softly. "I attend a science academy. It's not my idea; my parents are brainiacs and they make me go—"

"What does this have to do with **F.A.R.T.**?" snapped Crabapple.

"I'll get there, Ms. Bossy Boots."

It took a lot for Apricot to show her fangs, but Crabapple had a way with people.

"There was an awards breakfast at school," continued Apricot. "All our parents were there, and all the usual kids won trophies, which is okay. Everyone clapped and smiled, including the parents of kids like me who didn't win anything, but something in their eyes—in my parents' eyes—said, *Why isn't my kid like that? What did we do wrong?*"

"Like you're messed up because they messed up?" asked Banana.

"Exactly. And at that moment my parents would have given anything to have a **F.A.R.T.** manual or something like it. And I bet they're not alone. "

"I think my parents are pretty happy with me," said Banana

as he paged through the cookbook. "Sure, I get the usual 'Stop texting in the shower. Get off your computer. Get out of your room. You stink; take a shower. Being Friended doesn't mean you have friends. This is what soap looks like. Stop blogging. Why did you call the International Space Station on our house phone? Milk Duds are not breakfast. Stop wearing the same shirt. Who did you sell your bed to? Minecraft isn't a career. Why did you mail your shoes to Detroit? Don't you hear your alarm? Read a book—this book, any book.' . . . Now that you mention it, yeah, my parents would love a **F.A.R.T.** manual."

Apricot turned to Crabapple. "Where do you stand on **F.A.R.T.**?"

Of all the Only Onlys, I needed Crabapple to believe me, because people believe her. They don't like her, but that's what you get for being a great reporter forever chasing the BIG story. The question was: Did **F.A.R.T.** rate as a Big Story?

"Look," she began, "I agree that some parents would love a **F.A.R.T.** manual, but logically, how could **F.A.R.T.** exist without anyone finding out? Anyway, we have no proof."

"We have Popcorn's word," said Apricot.

"It's not enough. I need facts," said Crabapple. "I'm a reporter."

45

"You're an Only Only."

"It's still not enough."

"Crabapple's right," I said. "It's not enough."

Banana and Apricot looked thrown by my remark, but they held back. They knew me.

"So what if we all scream about **F.A.R.T.**?" I continued. "We're kids. Who's going to believe us? We've got no money, no cars, no jobs, no credit cards, no vote . . . nothing. And parents? They've got it all. And they're everywhere. No, I agree with Crabapple—this is too big for us."

"Just a second." Crabapple raised her finger. "All I said was—"

"You said that we need evidence, and you're right—but we'll never get it. We don't have the skills, the guts, the brains—"

"I didn't say—"

"Of course, if we *did* get some evidence, a manual or something, it would be more than a great news story. It would bring freedom, hope, and yes, a new day to kids everywhere."

"Oh, that's beautiful, Popcorn," said Apricot.

"Solid," said Banana.

"Thank you, my friends, but that day will never come, and do you know why?"

"WHO DOESN'T HAVE THE BRAINS?" Crabapple had taken the bait. It was time to reel her in.

"I didn't mean you," I lied.

"Certainly not you," agreed Apricot, who gave me a sly wink.

"Well, all right, then," huffed Crabapple. "Any rookie reporter could solve this. Nothing's impossible if you know how to use the right tools, and I do. If there's proof that **F.A.R.T.** exists, then we will find it. If there's proof that it does *not* exist, then we will find that, too."

"WE"—it was the magic word I'd been hoping for.

DIARY 8
DAY OF THE DUMPSTER

wo days ago I got punk'd by a cookbook that used to be a **F.A.R.T.** manual. Today I'm in a dumpster along with the other Only Onlys. This is progress, and I'll tell you why.

Crabapple had put on her Bossy Boots—as Apricot called them—and given each of us our marching orders. She had Banana analyze my computer for hackers who might have wiped my ViewTube channel. Apricot had the job of slogging through her parents' science library for a hidden **F.A.R.T.** manual. For her part, Crabapple vowed to find a confidential source inside **F.A.R.T.** who would give her an exclusive interview. (How she would manage this I had no idea.) When I asked her what I was supposed to do, she replied, "Your chemistry project. By yourself."

Just the same, I had one clue left to follow, but first, there was this dumpster assignment I told you about. See, Banana had sent us all a message on a secret **F.A.R.T. WIKI** that he'd created:

> Banana: Everyone, meet me in the dumpster behind Generic Computer Corporation downtown ASAP. Bring gloves. Wear boots. You'll see.
>
> Apricot: Did you say IN the dumpster?
>
> Popcorn: I'll follow you anywhere, dude!
>
> Crabapple: On my way!

Once in the dumpster, our task was simple: Banana would point at a junked computer part—a damaged disc drive or a crushed keyboard—and we would fetch. The trick was to separate it from leftover lunches and the creepy crawlies that fed on them.

"Eeeew, this garbage reeks!" cried Apricot. "And some of it's moving!"

Banana winced. "Garbage? One day this will all be in a museum."

"So will your shirt," said Crabapple.

I examined a mouse pad covered in mustard, emblazoned

49

with the words *Generic Computers. A Name You Can Trust.* "Banana, I still don't get it. How does this help us find **F.A.R.T.**?"

"I scanned your computer," he replied, "and you were definitely hacked. Whoever did it escaped into a part of the internet where search engines don't go. Some of those websites don't even have addresses. The good news is, they left a Hansel and Gretel."

He smiled at my confusion. He clearly enjoyed being the smartest guy in the dumpster.

"It's a trail that led to this." Banana punched up a **F.A.R.T.WIKI** posting on his phone.

>ACCESS RESTRICTED * ACCESS RESTRICTED * ACCESS RESTRICTED
>Portal #6 Fatal Error Run code loop resend
>Enter Password:_____

"It's a portal to the hackers' website."

"Is it **F.A.R.T.**'s?" I asked.

"I think so. It's kind of wonky, though. They're using an ancient programming language, as if they built the site a long time ago."

"Can you speak this language?"

"Dude, it's what I do, but I need an ancient computer to do it." He opened his backpack and revealed our swag so far. "We've got an original Mac, and we're mating it to a Radio Shack TRS-80, a Commodore Amiga, a Bowmar Brain, a Cray-2, a Coleco Adam, a Univac 60, and . . ."

Apricot raised her hand. "May I interrupt?" (She was always the politest Squid Kid.) "If any of those components proves unreliable, use an emulator to re-create the original computer environment without the actual hardware."

We all stopped and stared at her. "Wow. How'd you come up with that?" I asked.

Her face flushed red. "Sorry, searching through my parents' science books is getting to me."

"I could listen to you guys for hours," said Crabapple, "but isn't all of this pointless if we don't have a password?"

I agreed. "If this is a website for parents, they'd want something easy to remember, right? Mine use 1-2-3-4."

"How about something that might remind them of the word **F.A.R.T.**?" suggested Apricot.

"Good idea. I'll brainstorm it at the library," said Crabapple as she jotted notes on her pad.

Meanwhile, Apricot stood behind her and mouthed to me:

Bossy Boots likes you! I must have made a goofy face, because Crabapple spun around to catch her in the act, but instead she saw Apricot examining a spiky ball that she'd pulled from the rubble. She dangled it by its cord and said, "Hey, Banana, what's this?"

Banana's eyes widened into scooter pies. "Apricot! Be careful. Don't move. That's a Volt Hammer! Those things were outlawed years ago."

"Yeeeech!" Apricot freaked and tossed it to me like a hot potato, and I would have caught it if the 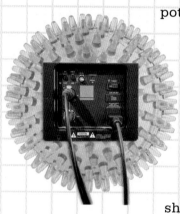 floor hadn't tilted out from under me, sending us all into a pile of packing peanuts. The walls around us began to shudder and the wheels below us rumbled. Blinding sunlight filled the dumpster as the shade of the Generic Computer Corporation building slid away.

We were moving. Somewhere. Fast.

The dumpster tossed us like a salad, but I managed to climb onto Banana's shoulders to see over its rim. I almost wish I hadn't. A large truck was towing us down the highway. A sign above its tailgate read:

CRAZY DAVEY'S
COMPUTER ★ CRUNCHERS
Recycle your bytes into bucks!

So that was it. We were on our way to be crunched by a guy named "Crazy Davey."

What a perfect time to panic.

I waved like mad at a car traveling beside us. A little kid inside saw me and started screaming and pointing, but it didn't matter. His mother, who was driving and texting and eating and talking, leaned back and corked his mouth with a juice box. That was that.

The dumpster picked up speed as we left the city limits and approached the highway. I don't know about you, but going seventy-five miles per hour in a garbage can was not on my bucket list.

"How do we stop this thing?" I shouted down to Banana.

"What's the name of the street we're on?" he yelled back.

I told him, and within seconds our steel prison screeched to a halt, launching me off Banana's shoulders and into a pile of moldy motherboards.

"Thank heavens he stopped," gasped Apricot.

"Thank Traffic Boss!" said Banana as he pointed to an app on his phone. "It changes traffic lights. I made it myself."

What a great app for Driver's Ed, I thought.

With the dumpster at a standstill, we pulled each other out, but Banana stayed behind. "I'm fine," he yelled as the truck pulled away. "I live by the dump. This is perfect for me."

As Banana faded into the distance, a pinging text on Crabapple's phone brought a smile to her face.

"Yes!" she shouted as she tapped out a reply. "I may have landed my informer inside **F.A.R.T.**! I gotta go."

Before I could ask her anything, she dashed across the street toward a bus that was lurching forward.

"There's no way she can make that bus," said Apricot to me.

"Wanna bet?"

Crabapple ran alongside and pounded under the bus driver's window until he hit the brakes and let her on. Even after boarding the bus, she stared him down for daring to get between her and a Big Story.

"I can't imagine Crabapple's parents ever wanting a **F.A.R.T.** manual," said Apricot as we watched the bus pull away. "She's smart, she knows what she wants, and she lets nothing stand in her way. I mean, she's perfect."

"Maybe she's perfect *because* her parents use a **F.A.R.T.** manual," I said.

Apricot cocked her head at me like a confused puppy. "Do you think so?"

"Apricot, I am in a world of **F.A.R.T.** I don't know what I'm saying anymore."

"What are you going to do now?"

"Follow a hunch," I replied, "but it can't possibly lead any-where. How about you?"

"I'll follow you."

DIARY 9
MADAM PAKLAVA KNOWS ALL

Apricot gently sang "The Wheels on the Bus" as the wheels on our bus took us closer, I hoped, to another piece of the **F.A.R.T.** puzzle, though it would be a miracle if Madam Paklava still worked in the same place after all these years.

Who's Madam Paklava? you ask.

Remember that rapper my parents invented when I caught them talking about **F.A.R.T.**—Fart Za-Lot Ubetcha? His Googol result had a playlist that I later posted on the **F.A.R.T.WIKI**. The songs all stink (naturally), but one didn't fit: "Madam Paklava Knows All."

The name "Madam Paklava" didn't register with me at first, but then I remembered a frightened little kid giving a dime to a mysterious old lady in return for telling his fortune. I was that kid, and the old lady was Madam Paklava.

That's who we were going to see.

"Do you think that she's still alive after all these years?" asked Apricot.

"She can never die," I replied.

Apricot smiled at my curious answer and then retreated into her own thoughts, watching the streets grow narrower and the neighborhoods less familiar. Finally she said, "Popcorn, I'm thinking of something that's so frightening, I'm afraid to say it."

"Why? They're only words."

She shifted uncomfortably in her seat. "I once read that when you say something, you put words out into the universe. And words mean things. They're like magnets. They attract other people's thoughts and ideas and pretty soon, whatever you were thinking can become real. I believe that. Do you?"

"I don't know, but whatever you tell me, I won't share with the universe."

She took a deep breath and relaxed. "Okay," she began, "what if some kids *know* that their parents are using a **F.A.R.T.** manual to control them, but they're okay with it?"

57

"What kids would do that?"

"Oh, kids with the Disease to Please? Kids who'd rather make their parents happy instead of just being themselves. I know kids like that." She looked out the window and murmured, "I'm like that . . . sometimes."

"But to surrender completely to **F.A.R.T.**?" I said. "Nah. No way. No kid would."

"Popcorn, what if your parents said, 'Look, if you let us use this **F.A.R.T.** manual on you, you'll get perfect grades, we'll never bother you, you'll go to a great college, and someday you'll make a lot of money.' What would you do?"

"Last stop!" shouted the driver as the bus hissed to a stop.

The sign was as big as a house. "Smiley's Retro Arcade?" asked Apricot. "This is where Madam Paklava works?"

"She used to," I replied. "My father used to take me here."

Ringing bells and clanking tokens welcomed us as we entered this kid-legal casino full of Skee-Ball, pinball, and claw machines unable to hold on to a prize. Yee-ha! You could practically smell the lunch money going up in smoke. As we searched for Madam Paklava, we saw kids earning points for prizes like joy buzzers ("Scare your friends!"), fake blood ("Scare your mom!"), and wax lips ("Scare your dentist!"). The super-big prizes like an electric guitar and a complete set of Pogs (?) were forever unwon, just as they were when I was a kid. You'd have a better shot at visiting Banana's Club Med on the moon than winning those treasures.

I pointed toward the end of a row of video games that included *Pong* and *Pac-Man* and cheered, "There she is! Right where I left her!"

MADAM PAKLAVA KNOWS ALL

said the sign above a dummy fortune-teller trapped in an old display case. She was hunched over a table with the tools of her trade spread before her—playing cards, a crystal ball, and a rabbit's foot.

"You know what I used to wonder?" I asked.

"You wondered how she went to the bathroom."

"How'd you know?"

She shrugged. "Boys."

I dropped a dime into a brass slot and stood back. Nothing happened at first, but then the old wooden box began to hum and a dusty light bulb inside the cabinet flickered to awaken Madam from her hibernation. Her plastic hand hovered to and fro over the glass ball and her rickety head jerked from side to side as if she were reading the faded cards before her. Then we heard the cackling voice of a drowning witch from a broken speaker: "For the price of a dime, I'll give you this rhyme, and a prediction that's stranger than fiction. Heed what I say, then be on your way."

"Cranky, isn't she?" said Apricot. "Maybe she does need a bathroom break."

Madam Paklava inched back to her original pose and froze, the light flickered out, and a fortune card slithered out of the cabinet like a flattened yellow snake.

Apricot nodded in admiration. "Not bad for ten cents."

We read the card over and over, but if there was a clue about

F.A.R.T. in this lame fortune about "trust" and "career," we couldn't see it. I posted the fortune card on the **F.A.R.T. WIKI** in case Banana or Crabapple could figure it out.

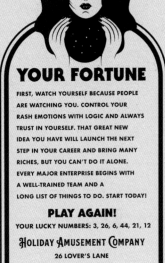

MADAM PAKLAVA

YOUR FORTUNE

FIRST, WATCH YOURSELF BECAUSE PEOPLE ARE WATCHING YOU. CONTROL YOUR RASH EMOTIONS WITH LOGIC AND ALWAYS TRUST IN YOURSELF. THAT GREAT NEW IDEA YOU HAVE WILL LAUNCH THE NEXT STEP IN YOUR CAREER AND BRING MANY RICHES, BUT YOU CAN'T DO IT ALONE. EVERY MAJOR ENTERPRISE BEGINS WITH A WELL-TRAINED TEAM AND A LONG LIST OF THINGS TO DO. START TODAY!

PLAY AGAIN!
YOUR LUCKY NUMBERS: 3, 26, 6, 44, 21, 12

HOLIDAY AMUSEMENT COMPANY
26 LOVER'S LANE

Yet something bothered me about that fortune, something that only half my brain could see, but wasn't telling the other half.

"I'm sorry this was such a waste," I said. "Like I said, it was only a hunch. Why would **F.A.R.T.** be giving us clues, anyway?"

"Popcorn, playing your hunches is just believing in yourself. Oh, don't make that face. Remember how I used to talk about writing a book, but I couldn't see myself doing it? And you said, 'Sometimes ya just gotta believe'?"

"Yeah, I remember."

"Well, sometimes you do." She looked at her Hello Kitty watch and frowned. "Ugh! I've got science books to search."

We walked to the exit and figured out what bus she should take. As she turned to leave, she stopped and grabbed my arm. "Hey, don't forget to read my book!"

* * *

I couldn't resist hanging around Smiley's Retro Arcade a while longer. I squeezed the handle on a Love Tester that rated me **A DUD AS A STUD**, and rolled a perfect game of Skee-Ball. (I hadn't lost my touch!) The truth is, I had missed this place. I'd missed playing air hockey with my old man, eating funnel cake and puking in the parking lot, but that was a million years ago. Did my dad have a **F.A.R.T.** manual back then? And if I'd known about it, would I have cared?

"What would you do?" Apricot's question during our bus ride gnawed at me, but so did that fortune card.

PING!

Crabapple texted me on the **F.A.R.T. WIKI**.

CRABAPPLE: Popcorn, I'm about to make contact with a F.A.R.T. insider, but I need help NOW! (My location attached.)

I gave my Skee-Ball points to a little kid, who said, "Thanks, Mr. Man," and I hopped onto the next bus.

62

DIARY 10
HEY, PARENTS!

Pssst! Popcorn! Over here!"

I found Crabapple crouched behind a row of bushes near an empty soccer field at our municipal park. "Get down!" she hissed. "They'll see you!"

I dug in beside her and got a whiff of dumpster stink still lingering from that morning. She pushed a branch aside and squinted through a small pair of binoculars.

"*Who'll* see us?" I asked.

She checked her watch. "We've got ten minutes. Okay, here's the deal." She clicked on her **F.A.R.T.WIKI** app and passed me her phone. "Check this out."

It was an advertisement aimed at parents to buy their secret manual.

"OMG, who's running this ad?" I asked.

"I am," she said. "I figured the best way to find a parent who would inform on **F.A.R.T.** was to advertise for one. It's in today's PennySaver. You know, those free magazines you see outside supermarkets."

"So that text you got before was someone answering this ad. What happens next?"

She passed me the binoculars. "See that shoebox across the field?"

I did.

"Inside, there's a red envelope containing a hundred-dollar bill. I was told to leave it on top of that storm drain. Five minutes from now someone's going to take that money and leave a manual. Those were the instructions."

"You put a hundred-dollar bill inside that shoebox?" I said. "Seriously?"

"You can't put a price on a Big Story."

"Well, someone did." I passed the binoculars back.

"And that someone will be our line into **F.A.R.T.**," she said with quiet authority.

My spidey sense tingled. There wasn't a person in sight, and evening was creeping in.

"This could get dangerous."

"That's why you're here," she replied.

"Oh."

The Big Story; it was always the Big Story with her. I shouldn't complain. That's how I roped her into this, but who was she trying to impress with that Big Story? This wasn't just about getting into Journalism Camp. Her "Big Story" hang-up started long before that. In first grade she wrote a news story in their *Gopher Gazette* that doubted the tooth fairy. It put her entire class into grief counseling, but she didn't care—it was a Big Story. They paid her back by putting her on a No Valentines list, and she still didn't care. I guess having the Only Onlys in her back pocket gave her the courage to be so alone, but in the end, would any story be big enough for her, and for what?

She jiggled her watch. It glowed 4:59. "Any second now." She peered through the binoculars again. "No . . . wait! It moved. The box moved!"

"Are you sure? No one got near it."

"I'm sure," she said. "Let's go."

We charged across the field and opened the shoebox. The money was gone, but in its place was a paper bag sealed with tape.

Crabapple examined the box closely. "How did they switch the money for the manual?"

"I think someone hid in that storm drain, reached up from below, opened the box, took the money, and left that bag."

CLANG!

Across the field a man in a green cap had emerged from another storm drain, letting the metal grate fall behind him. In his hand was a red envelope.

"And that's the guy who did it," I said, pointing across the field.

Crabapple called to him. "Hey, I want to talk to you!"

The Green Cap guy looked at us and bolted. Crabapple took off after him. I grabbed the bag from the shoebox and ran after them both. We scurried across tennis courts, the jungle gym, T-ball practice, a kiddie birthday party, and a lacrosse field, and still the Green Cap guy remained one step ahead. As we ran, I managed to tear open the bag and look inside.

"Crabapple!" I panted.

"What?"

"This isn't the manual!"

"Well, what is it?"

"Because I Said So."

"Because you said *what*?"

"STOP RUNNING, WILL YA?"

We collapsed in a Little League dugout and gasped for air. My days of cutting gym and eating pork rinds for breakfast had finally caught up with me. Meanwhile, Green Cap scaled the outfield fence and escaped.

"There goes your hundred bucks," I said, "and for nothing."

"What do you mean?"

I emptied the bag onto the players' bench. Out poured a pair of glasses and a pamphlet entitled *Because I Said So*.

It claimed that you could control kids by putting on these hypno-glasses and saying, "Because I said so."

"This isn't the **F.A.R.T.** manual?" asked Crabapple.

"No, this is a scam," I replied. "Or, as my grandpa would say, 'We've been bamboozled.'"

"But we seemed so close," groaned Crabapple, tossing the silly specs aside.

"I'm sorry about the hundred bucks. I'll pay you back somehow."

"Forget it," she said. "I'm a reporter. It goes with the job."

"No, we're in this together. I won't blame you if you go back to your other story."

"What other story?"

"The one you were working on when I first called you," I said.

"Oh, that. I heard that our cafeteria was putting sawdust in the hamburgers to save money. If you've ever eaten them, you'd believe it. So I managed to get some raw meat from the school's freezer to have it tested."

"What happened?"

"Nothing. Some dunce at the lab ate it for lunch. That's when I went back to my newspaper adviser and pitched her the **F.A.R.T.** story," she said.

"Did she laugh at you?"

"No. It was weird. She got nasty, but in a nice way. She said that I was her first choice for Journalism Camp this summer, but that it's hard to recommend someone who chases fairy tales."

"**F.A.R.T.** is no fairy tale."

"So you say. Anyway, when I nail this story, it'll be too big for anyone to ignore." She picked up the so-called magic glasses from the dugout floor and examined them. "Hey, Popcorn?" There was a slight plea in her voice. "You really saw a **F.A.R.T.** manual at your parents' house . . . right?"

"Yup."

"How can you be so sure?"

I took the glasses from her and looked into her eyes. "Because I said so!"

She smiled. She didn't do it often, but it lit up her face like the rays of the setting sun that filled the dugout. Too bad it didn't last. A shadow engulfed us both and a voice thundered, "I've been bamboozled!"

The Green Cap guy that we'd chased around the park towered over us. He looked a lot bigger up close. "Where's my money?" he demanded. He took the hundred-dollar bill out of the red envelope and flung it at me.

It wasn't money that he'd thrown at me, but a coupon for Mike's Super-Duper Subs that *looked* like a hundred-dollar

bill. (By the way, try Mike's Hawaiian sub. It's awesome.)

"You gave him fake money?" I asked Crabapple.

"I didn't have a hundred dollars."

"If I had done this," I said, "you'd be giving me lectures about truth and honesty—"

"This was for journalism, not for junk food."

"And to think I actually felt sorry for you!"

"HEY!" bellowed the Green Cap guy. "Remember me? I want my money, then you two can go to the prom."

I had one idea. I'd seen others do it, but I'd never had the guts to try it myself. I stood up and waved my hand in his face and said: *"These are not the droids you're looking for."*

Luck comes in many forms.

In our case it was the baseball field's sprinkler system, which turned on and shot a stream of water up the guy's nose and, I swear, out his ears.

We bolted from that dugout like we'd won the World Series.

DIARY 11
F.A.R.T. HACKER

Just in case you were keeping score on how the Only Onlys were doing against **F.A.R.T.**, here's a rundown. First, we got trapped in a runaway dumpster and were *this close* to getting recycled.

Fart Za-Lot Ubetcha, a rapper who doesn't exist, led me to

ACTUAL SIZE!?!

a robot soothsayer who gave me a fortune that I still can't figure out. Banana was building a Franken-computer to hack into **F.A.R.T.**'s secret website. To keep him stoked, I sent him a Mammoth Malted Milk Ball from one of my old ViewTube sponsors. He was happy. Crabapple had blown a hundred bogus bucks on a bogus manual and hoped that landing the "big **F.A.R.T.** story" would win her a place in Journalism Camp. Apricot had read so many of her parents' science books that she started telling jokes like: "How do you organize a space party? You planet." (Get it? Of course you do. Now try to forget it.) Meanwhile, I was getting nowhere hunting for my parents' **F.A.R.T.** manual. Don't bother adding up the score. We were losing.

So, just when I thought that the light at the end of the tunnel was an oncoming train, Banana delivered some good news over the **F.A.R.T.WIKI**:

BANANA: Yo! Yo! Yo!—the computer's ready!

APRICOT:

POPCORN: Outstanding!

CRABAPPLE: When can we see it?

BANANA: NOW. IF you can find us a place that can handle high voltage. This thing is a beast!

CRABAPPLE: I know one place that might work. They used to sell smoothies.

POPCORN: Sounds tasty.

CRABAPPLE: Not these smoothies.

Crabapple found the perfect place for Banana to unveil his computer—a closed-up fast food joint called Clucky's Chicken Smoothies.

Within hours, we were ducking under a **NO TRESPASSING** barrier and unlocking a side door that led

inside the ghostly mall. Its main court was lined with dark and deserted stores like the Mall Cinema, which advertised the first Harry Potter flick, and Sneaker Planet, which had a sale on Shaq Attaqs. It was like time travel.

At the food court a six-foot statue of Clucky welcomed us to his "coop." Remember Clucky? He was the cartoon chicken who liked to drink chicken smoothies. (Pretty gagworthy, huh?) The high-voltage outlets that had once powered Clucky's poultry pulverizers were perfect for Banana's needs.

I can't say that we were dazzled when Banana unpacked his Franken-computer. It looked like a pile of dumpster junk (which it was) strung together by a thick data cable, but he adored it. "I call it **F.A.R.T. HACKER**," he said as he patted its circuit boards. "Beautiful, isn't it?"

"Yeah, it's gorgeous," said Crabapple impatiently. "Now, hurry up!"

Banana plugged it in and clicked a power switch that he'd poached from an Easy-Bake oven. **F.A.R.T. HACKER**'s ancient interconnected computers wheezed and huffed as they booted up. When an old-school prompt ">" blinked on the monitor, it was official: **F.A.R.T. HACKER** was alive!

"Good boy," said Banana to his creation. "Now, let's make history."

He typed commands so quickly on its old clickity-clackity keyboard that his hands were a blur. He didn't use a mouse. Mice hadn't been invented back when these computers were built. When "ACCESS DENIED" or "FATAL ERROR" stood in his way, he'd switch keyboards or pour a can of soda onto an overheating disc drive. A master was at work.

Our hearts stopped when this appeared on the screen:

```
Enter Password:_____
```

"What do we do now?" I asked.

"I'm going to run a random password generator," replied Banana. "It'll send out ten thousand guesses a second. We'll get a ping soon."

But an hour passed, and not one ping did we get.

"What else can we do?" I asked.

"Nothing," Banana said. "We wait."

"We can't wait forever," said Apricot.

I turned to Crabapple. "Weren't you going to research passwords at the library?"

"Yeah," she replied, "but it didn't work out. The research librarian gave me words associated with the word 'fart,' not **F.A.R.T.** the organization."

"Let's try them anyway," I said.

"They're too stupid to even repeat. It's what little kids say instead of the word 'fart.'"

"Nothing is too stupid for the Only Onlys," I said with pride.

Apricot and Banana nodded in agreement.

Crabapple groaned and flipped open her notebook. "The first one is 'trouser cough.'"

Banana typed it in and hit enter.

"PASSWORD INCORRECT" flashed on the screen.

"Next?" he asked.

"Bowel howl."

PASSWORD INCORRECT.

"Vapor caper."

PASSWORD INCORRECT.

"Funny foghorn."

PASSWORD INCORRECT.

"Backdoor bagpipe."

PASSWORD INCORRECT.

"Old-cheese Febreze."

PASSWORD INCORRECT.

"Steamin' the beans."

PASSWORD INCORRECT.

"Whiffy McBlatts."

PASSWORD INCORRECT.

"Yule log smog."

PASSWORD INCORRECT.

77

"Brutal bugle."

PASSWORD INCORRECT.

Crabapple closed her notebook. "This is getting us nowhere."

"Was that all of them?" I asked.

"No. There was one more, but I refuse to—"

"Say it!" demanded Apricot.

"*Peanut butter and smelly!*" Crabapple cried.

WELCOME

We were in.

DIARY 12
THIS CHANGES EVERYTHING

Banana and his **F.A.R.T. HACKER** had taken us into the most mysterious part of the internet; maybe inside **F.A.R.T.** itself. He hit enter again, and this came up:

FILE DIRECTORY

PRODUCTION

RESEARCH AND DEVELOPMENT

PURCHASING

MARKETING AND ADVERTISING

HUMAN RESOURCES

ADMINISTRATION AND MANAGEMENT

ACCOUNTING AND FINANCE

SALES DEPARTMENT

THE BRAIN MODEM

DISTRIBUTION

TECH SUPPORT

LEGAL DEPARTMENT

MANUFACTURING

WAREHOUSE AND STORAGE

"Where are we?" asked Apricot. "What are we looking at?"

"This is what a hacker would see," replied Banana. "It's a directory of hyperlinks—the skeleton that holds up a website."

"Is it **F.A.R.T.**?" asked Crabapple.

"Could be," he replied.

"Who else would use 'peanut butter and smelly' as their password?" asked Apricot.

Crabapple looked straight at me. "I can think of quite a few people."

"What's a Brain Modem?" I asked. "Second column, second row: 'The Brain Modem.'"

Banana clicked on it, and this zombie woman with oogie eyes appeared.

Then he clicked on her face.

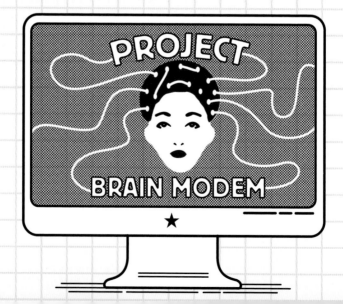

YES, it's coming!

PROJECT: BRAIN MODEM. Imagine a device that will make your child behave the way YOU want, when YOU want. Imagine never having to use a manual again. Imagine using your phone to control your child's behavior! Say hello to the BRAIN MODEM APP.

Using advances in electronic nerve research, the Brain Modem and its app will make putting GOOD behaviors into your child's brain as easy as putting garbage into a can, AND THEY WON'T EVEN KNOW YOU'RE DOING IT!

Are we there yet? Almost. Brain Modem research has consumed us for many years, but the results were FAIL CITY. The big problem was the brain interface. (See left.)

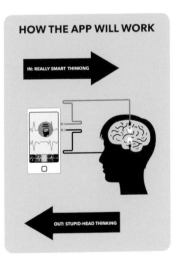

HOW THE APP WILL WORK

IN: REALLY SMART THINKING

OUT: STUPID-HEAD THINKING

Here's the BIG NEWS: We have found a NEW WAY INTO THE BRAIN, and we will begin testing it IMMEDIATELY. Would you like your child to be part of this new test? Click on the <u>CHART</u> on the next page. You'll see times and places where you can sign up so that YOU can be a part of this revolution.

The web page lingered for a few seconds, and then this message appeared:

UNAUTHORIZED TRANSMISSION TERMINATED.

DO NOT COME BACK.

Banana spoke for us all when he said, "Oh yeah? Well, bite me."

On that note, **F.A.R.T. HACKER**'s fuses blew.

DIARY 13
THE BRAIN MODEM

A Brain Modem? Mind control?" said Apricot. "Is that what **F.A.R.T.** is into?"

"Banana, can you get that website back?" I asked.

He shook his head. "**F.A.R.T. HACKER**'s fried for now." He unplugged its roasted connections with a pot holder he'd found at Clucky's.

"This is worse than a **F.A.R.T.** manual," said Apricot. "It's lazy. Kids won't clean their room? Zap 'em with the Brain Modem. Didn't get the child you hoped for? Reboot 'em!"

"I think it's awesome," said Banana, "in a bad way, of course. I wonder when they're going to test it on kids?"

"Maybe they already have," I said.

"Stop," said Crabapple firmly. "Let's all take a breath. None of us actually saw the word '**F.A.R.T.**,' right? This could have been a medical website or someone writing a horror story."

"Yeah, well, it's a good one," said Apricot.

"It could even be a joke," continued Crabapple. "It could be George Washington on the *Titanic* again or—"

"Crabapple!" a voice boomed across the food court. "What are you doing here? Who are those children?"

We were busted. Crabapple's mother and some business guy in a suit were walking toward us. I guess she was trying to sell him this mall, but what was our excuse for being there? And with **F.A.R.T. HACKER**, no less?

Crabapple turned to us and said, "I'll handle this." She walked confidently up to her mother and announced: "These are not children. These are real estate clients of mine. Allow me to present Dr. Palomitas, Dr. Plátano, and their translator . . . Apricotia."

Now THIS is going to be interesting, I thought.

The guy suddenly seemed worried. "You didn't tell me you were showing this place to anyone else," he said to Crabapple's mom.

Her mother peered at us over Crabapple's shoulder.

"Oh, they're just kids," she assured him. Then she bored into Crabapple. "And I'm sure that my daughter will tell us what in the world they are doing here, WON'T YOU."

"Why, certainly," replied Crabapple. "Have you heard of Instagram? Twitter? Snapchat? Well, these 'kids,' as you call them, are working on something bigger."

The guy squinted at us. "Palomitas and Plátano? That sounds familiar."

It should sound familiar, suit boy, I thought. It was the name of the restaurant behind him.

PALOMITAS & PLÁTANOS
MEXICAN RESTAURANT

"What are they working on?" he asked.

"I'm not allowed to say," replied Crabapple, "but imagine . . . adding aromas to your texts."

Banana quickly grabbed a Magic Marker and wrote the words "Cell Smell" on his wrist, no doubt the name of his next app.

"But why are they here?" asked her mother.

"Why are they here?" repeated Crabapple, treading water.

I suppose I should have said something, but she was so much fun to watch.

"They're here to test this mall's electrical outlets," she said finally.

"Why would they do that?"

"Why? Yeah, why. Because they want to buy this place and turn it into a new tech hub like Silicon Valley."

The business guy's eyes lit up. "We need to talk," he said to Crabapple's mother, "and I'd like your daughter to join us."

As the three of them retreated to the opposite end of the food court, I whispered to Apricot and Banana, "Let's hope that guy doesn't Googol us."

We stuffed **F.A.R.T. HACKER** into duffel bags as fast as we could, although Banana couldn't resist grabbing old packets of Clucky's Secret Sauce.

A short time later, Crabapple walked back to us alone, her eyes fixed to the ceiling.

"What's she looking at?" asked Banana.

"Nothing," said Apricot. "She's pushing tears back into her head."

"I just sold this mall," she announced to us.

"To us?" I asked.

"Not to you, dummy. To that guy with my mom. He was afraid that you'd beat him to it."

"Congrats!" said Banana. "Are the smoothies coming back? I've got lots of secret sauce."

"*I* didn't sell it," she replied. "My mother says I sold it. She says she couldn't have done it without me. She also said that real estate is in my blood. That I'm going to intern at her office this summer."

"Well, you did sell a whole mall," I said.

"I don't want to sell anything! You sound like my parents. 'Be nicer. Make some friends. Today's friends are tomorrow's customers. Build your brand. Network. Stop writing about things that don't concern you. Didn't you learn anything from that tooth fairy mess?' Well, I'm not a brand. I'm a reporter. And I don't want to sell old houses this summer; I want to go to Journalism Camp."

"So go," said Apricot.

"I can't. Not without a Big Story. *This* story. This completely ridiculous, knuckleheaded story about **F.A.R.T.** and Brain Modems and who knows what else."

She dropped to the floor beside the statue of Clucky and folded her knees to her chin. The Perfect Daughter—that's what Apricot had called her. I guess perfect isn't enough for some parents. At least I knew who Crabapple was trying to impress with that Big Story for all these years.

Apricot sat down beside her and squeezed her arm. "Crabapple, write the **F.A.R.T.** story. Do it now. Kids have got to know about the Brain Modem before it's too late."

"But we still have no facts."

"The facts will come later." Then Apricot smiled at me. "Sometimes ya just gotta believe."

DIARY 14
ONE OF OUR ONLY ONLYS
IS MISSING

My first day back at school after learning about the Brain Modem was pure frustration.

All I wanted to do was sneak onto the principal's PA system and scream *THE BRAIN MODEM IS COMING!*, but even if I could, what good would it do? When I'd talked about **F.A.R.T.** before, my classmates laughed me out of homeroom. If I ranted about a Brain Modem, they'd give me a first-class ticket to Candy Land. Crabapple (as usual) was right; we needed proof.

Luckily, these **F.A.R.T. WIKI** posts gave me hope.

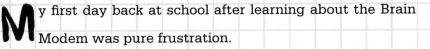 **APRICOT**: HEY! I think I've found the manual!!! One of my parents' books is titled: *The Effects of Potassium and Iodine on*

Darmstadtium When Bonded to Oxygen, Beryllium, and Yttrium in an Environment of Nobelium and Tungsten. It was so simple!

POPCORN: Huh? 🤔

CRABAPPLE: Double huh?

APRICOT: I matched the elements in the book's title to the periodic table. (See right.)

CRABAPPLE: Clever you. Did you read the book?

APRICOT: I can't. It's in a glass case that's locked. It's controlled by Wi-Fi.

19 **K** Potassium	53 **I** Iodine	110 **D** Darmstad
8 **O** Oxygen	4 **Be** Beryllium	39 **Y** Yttriu
102 **No** Nobelium	74 **W** Tungsten	

BANANA: NP. I've got an app for that. Lock Rocket. I'll send you the link.

APRICOT: Thanks! I'll keep you posted!

Days passed, but we heard nothing more from Apricot. No texts. No postings. Nothing. Meanwhile, Crabapple wrote the first few paragraphs of her "big" **F.A.R.T.** story and posted it on the **F.A.R.T. WIKI**.

"Time to Believe"

by Crabapple

There are people who still believe that planet Earth is flat. They are wrong. There are people who believe that we never went to the moon. They are wrong. There are people who believe that an international conspiracy of parents dedicated to the obedience of children, called **F.A.R.T.** (Families Against Rotten Teens), could never exist.

They are wrong.

Since families began, parents have sought to control their children in various ways, but nothing comes close to the Brain Modem, an app that dives directly into a person's mind. With the push of a button, the Brain Modem promises to turn rambunctious rascals into obedient sheep.

There it was—the beginning of the Big Story she'd always wanted, written totally on faith. It was a very un-Crabapple thing to do. Once we got proof of **F.A.R.T.**, her school newspaper would have to publish it, I'm sure.

When I got Banana's text, I really felt that things were breaking our way:

91

BANANA: I've got a surprise for F.A.R.T. A big one. F.A.R.T. HACKER 2 IS READY TO LAUNCH THIS SATURDAY! It's bigger and badder than ever! Be at my house at noon. Parents out all day. BTW, has anyone heard from Apricot? I'm really worried.

We were all worried about Apricot. None of us went to the same school or lived in the same neighborhood, so for the moment, we could only guess what had happened to her. Banana even mapped our cell phones on the **F.A.R.T.WIKI**, but she was not to be found.

Had she discovered a **F.A.R.T.** manual in her home? Had she read it? Had her parents found out about it? I thought back to her words on the bus, about kids accepting **F.A.R.T.** to please their parents and get other goodies—"The Disease to Please," she called it. There was no way she'd do that, but when you added the Brain Modem into the mix, anything was possible.

DIARY 15
A SECRET HISTORY LESSON

I woke up early on Saturday so I could stop by Apricot's house before seeing Banana's new and improved **F.A.R.T. HACKER**. It was over a week ago that Apricot claimed to have found a **F.A.R.T.** manual in her parent's library, and we hadn't heard from her since.

I made a point of taking her book of poetry with me so she could autograph it like a big-time author. She'd like that. As I stuffed it into my backpack, something odd caught my eye. The first letter of each line in the title spelled out a word: *O-N-L-Y*. That was obvious, but where had I seen this kind of thing before?

As if to answer me, a ghastly voice cut through the usual

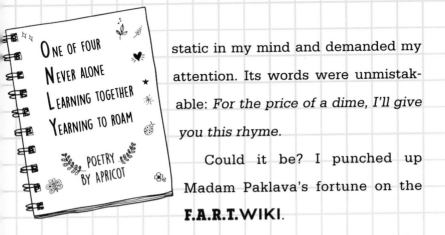

ONE OF FOUR
NEVER ALONE
LEARNING TOGETHER
YEARNING TO ROAM

POETRY
BY APRICOT

static in my mind and demanded my attention. Its words were unmistakable: *For the price of a dime, I'll give you this rhyme.*

Could it be? I punched up Madam Paklava's fortune on the **F.A.R.T. WIKI**.

WHAM! There it was. The first letter of every line of the card spelled out: "**F.A.R.T. IS REAL**."

Not only did the card list a nearby address, but it also told me what I desperately needed to hear: the Only Onlys were not alone.

MADAM PAKLAVA

YOUR FORTUNE

FIRST, WATCH YOURSELF BECAUSE PEOPLE
ARE WATCHING YOU. CONTROL YOUR
RASH EMOTIONS WITH LOGIC AND ALWAYS
TRUST IN YOURSELF. THAT GREAT NEW
IDEA YOU HAVE WILL LAUNCH THE NEXT
STEP IN YOUR CAREER AND BRING MANY
RICHES, BUT YOU CAN'T DO IT ALONE.
EVERY MAJOR ENTERPRISE BEGINS WITH
A WELL-TRAINED TEAM AND A
LONG LIST OF THINGS TO DO. START TODAY!

PLAY AGAIN!

YOUR LUCKY NUMBERS: 3, 26, 6, 44, 21, 12

ℋoliday Amusement Company

26 LOVER'S LANE

YOUR FORTU

FIRST, WATCH YOURSELF BECAUSE PE
ARE WATCHING YOU. CONTROL YOU
RASH EMOTIONS WITH LOGIC AND A
TRUST IN YOURSELF. THAT GREAT NE
IDEA YOU HAVE WILL LAUNCH THE N
STEP IN YOUR CAREER AND BRING M
RICHES, BUT YOU CAN'T DO IT ALON
EVERY MAJOR ENTERPRISE BEGINS W
AWELL-TRAINED TEAM AND A
LONG LIST OF THINGS TO DO. START

I practically busted the trucks of my skateboard getting to 26 Lover's Lane, the address on Madam Paklava's fortune card. The house was in one of those Sims Communities where every cottage looks the same, although you couldn't miss the sign nailed to the mailbox at #26.

> # 26 Lover's Lane
> # Home of Dr. Xavier Clabby
> # The World's Most Successful Author

I'd never heard of Xavier Clabby, "The World's Most Successful Author," but I wasn't the world's most successful reader, either. To avoid looking like some dweeb teen, I stuck the pot-roast-flavored gum that I was chewing—an experimental flavor from one of my ViewTube sponsors—under his mailbox. Then I concocted a brilliant cover story as to why I was knocking on his door. After all, the first thing you say to a stranger cannot be "**F.A.R.T.**"

As the door opened, I regretted slacking off in English class, because I'll never find the right words to describe Dr. Clabby. Imagine Sir Topham Hatt in an XXL tracksuit wearing a baseball cap emblazoned with the words: **IS YOUR ADVERTISING FLABBY? CALL DR. CLABBY!**

"May I help you?" he asked.

"Good day to you, sir," I said cheerfully. "I'm conducting a survey for *Skateboarders without Wheels*."

"My dear boy, wouldn't a skateboard without wheels be a snowboard?"

". . . Yeah."

"So, which is it? Do you represent snowboards, or skateboards?"

"Uh . . . Good day to you, sir—"

"WHO SENT YOU?"

"Madam Paklava."

A smile lit up his fleshy face. "Madam Paklava! Why didn't you say so? I've been writing her stuff for years. People make up silly excuses to meet me because I'm a celebrity, but the direct approach is always best, don't you think?"

"Sure."

He beckoned for me to enter. "Would you like to see my greatest hits, as I call them?"

I stepped inside the tiny cottage, but I wedged my skateboard against the door so that it stayed open. You never know.

He pointed with pride to the bumper stickers, banners, T-shirts, posters, signs, pens, badges, and buttons that filled his living room wall, each one telling you how to vote, eat, live, buy, think, and everything else.

"All that you see, I wrote," he said. "Ever hear of 'Take a bite out of crime'? Mine. Or 'Cross at the green, not in between'? Mine. How about 'Just do it'?"

"Isn't that Nike's?" I asked.

"It's mine, but they won't admit it. I've hired a lawyer. They'll be sorry."

"About Madam Paklava," I said, "there's one fortune you wrote that I really liked."

"Oh? Which one?" asked Clabby.

"'*F.A.R.T. IS REAL*.'"

He clutched his chest. "**F.A.R.T. IS REAL**? Heavens to Betsy! How shocking! I'd never put a cheap laugh like that into one of her fortunes."

"Yes, you did." I took the Madam Paklava card out of my pocket and handed it to him.

MADAM PAKLAV

YOUR FORTUNE

FIRST, WATCH YOURSELF BECAUSE PEOPLE ARE WATCHING YOU. CONTROL YOUR RASH EMOTIONS WITH LOGIC AND ALWAYS TRUST IN YOURSELF. THAT GREAT NEW IDEA YOU HAVE WILL LAUNCH THE NEXT STEP IN YOUR CAREER AND BRING MANY RICHES, BUT YOU CAN'T DO IT ALONE. EVERY MAJOR ENTERPRISE BEGINS WITH A WELL-TRAINED TEAM AND A LONG LIST OF THINGS TO DO. START TODAY!

PLAY AGAIN!
YOUR LUCKY NUMBERS: 3, 26, 6, 44, 21, 12

HOLIDAY AMUSEMENT COMPANY
26 LOVER'S LANE

"Why did you do it?" I persisted. "What did you mean, **F.A.R.T. IS REAL**?"

He studied the card, and then he studied me, as if to size me up.

"It doesn't mean anything," he said, tossing the card aside. "I admit it. It was a joke. Ha. Ha. Ha. See? I'm laughing."

"I don't think you were joking, Dr. Clabby. I think you know that **F.A.R.T.** stands for Families Against Rotten Teens, a super-secret organization of parents."

I was prepared for Clabby to push me out the door, but instead, he deflated into an easy chair and popped a Hydrox into his mouth. After a few thoughtful crunches, he looked at me and smiled. "You're quite right. I do know about **F.A.R.T.**"

"Are you a parent?" I asked.

"I'm a writer," he replied, "but to be a great writer you've got to read, so I read everything. Old books. Newspapers. You name it. Now, every once in a while I'll come across a reference to **F.A.R.T.** It's rare, but it happens. When it does, I cut it out and stash it in my **F.A.R.T.** file."

Clabby stood and opened a tall metal filing cabinet, which disturbed a caged blue parrot sitting on top of it. "Fart is real! Fart is real!" it squawked.

Fart is **REAL!**
Fart is **REAL!**

"Quiet, Mrs. Puckowitz!" shouted Clabby as he refilled her feeding tray. "I named her after my landlady," he explained. "A wonderful woman, except when the rent is due."

He dug deep into the cabinet and retrieved a bulging file that he emptied onto his dining table. "My **F.A.R.T.** file. I've never shared it with anyone."

It was breathtaking! Old pictures, torn-out pages, and newspaper clippings were spread out before me, each with a little bit of **F.A.R.T.**'s secret history. Clabby even had illustrations from old history books that had later been taken off the market.

There were also stories about kids who had learned about **F.A.R.T.** but couldn't come up with any proof.

The one thing that Clabby didn't have was an actual manual. When I told him about the one that I'd found and lost, it bothered him as much as it did me. I didn't tell him about the Brain Modem. I didn't want to go too far and fast with him.

I finally asked him why he put that secret message in

President Teddy Roosevelt gets his daily dose of F.A.R.T.

Caesar Salad, founder of F.A.R.T.

Henry the VIII, merciless ruler and dad

Madam Paklava's fortune card in the first place.

The question seemed to embarrass him. "Although I'm an incredible talent," he said matter-of-factly, "I'm also human. It's hard to keep as big a secret as **F.A.R.T.** to yourself. That's why I place hints about it into my writings. It helps, but honestly, I've wanted to talk to someone about **F.A.R.T.** for a long time."

"A friend of mine is a news reporter," I told him. "Will you tell her your story?"

He shook his head. "Dropping hints about **F.A.R.T.** in a fortune card is one thing, but attacking them in public is another. I once mentioned them in a blog, and my whole website vanished the next day. They have a security apparatus that deals harshly with whistleblowers like me."

"You mean the Plumbers?" I asked.

His eyes widened. "You are well informed, young man. Yes, the Plumbers. And between you and me, I hope I never meet them."

I understood. I knew the pain of taking on **F.A.R.T.** by myself.

"Dr. Clabby, if you share your story and your files, I promise that we'll see this through together—you, me, and my friends. Aren't you tired of going this alone?"

"I am," he said wearily.

"Take a chance with us. Sometimes ya just gotta believe."

"'Ya just gotta believe'? Hmm. I think I wrote that," he said. "Okay, include me in. Can you stop by later this afternoon? I need to get some parrot feed for Mrs. Puckowitz."

We shook hands and I left quickly before he changed his mind. As much as I had wanted to, there was no time to stop at Apricot's, so I went directly to Banana's house for the launching of **F.A.R.T. HACKER 2**. With any luck, Apricot might have gotten our messages and was already there.

DIARY 16
F.A.R.T. HACKER 2

Crabapple paced like a worried penguin in front of Banana's house.

"You're late," she said as I rode up to the front door.

I hopped off my skateboard, stomped on its tail, and caught the board in flight.

"Cheer up," I told her. "I've got something to tell you." The news about Clabby was bursting my insides.

"Yeah? Well, I've got something to tell you."

"Is it about Apricot? Is she here?"

Crabapple shook her head. "It's about something else."

Banana called to us from the backyard. "Yo! A little help here? Quick!"

We found him sitting at the heart of his new creation, **F.A.R.T. HACKER 2**, or **FH2**, as he called it. Three keyboards, six monitors, and a dozen open cans of sardines, chili, and Spaghetti Ready! surrounded him. He must have pulled an all-nighter working on his baby. Thank heaven for 7-Eleven.

FH2 had more computers, servers, and cables than the original, plus that Volt Hammer thingy that Banana had warned us about in the dumpster. This was the surprise he had in mind for **F.A.R.T.** The Volt Hammer pulsed with a Mello Yello glow and growled a hungry *oooga-oooga* sound. He said it was like a turbocharger for computers that would give **FH2** the added punch it needed to flatten **F.A.R.T.**'s defenses.

"Didn't you say that the Volt Hammer was dangerous?" I asked.

Banana fiddled with the dials on the mysterious spiky device. "No, I said it was outlawed. It was considered insanely unstable, but that's because people didn't know how to use it."

"Do you know how to use it?"

"Pretty much."

"That's good enough for me!" I said, keeping the vibe positive.

Banana gulped a spoonful of cold Spaghetti Ready! and

settled in for battle. "Okay, Crabapple, watch that hertz meter. Warn me if it goes over sixty. Popcorn, shout if the Volt Hammer glows anything but yellow."

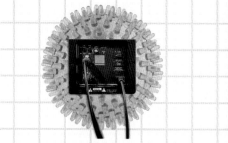

Banana's fingers danced over the keyboards as he retraced his steps to the password page. "I'm engaging the Volt Hammer . . . NOW!" he shouted.

"Are we in yet?" I asked. "The Hammer just changed from yellow to orange."

"Almost there. We're knocking on their back door!" He typed even faster, but then he stopped. "Uh-oh."

"What's *uh-oh*?" I asked.

"Look at the monitor," he said.

YOU SHOULD NOT HAVE RETURNED. WE WARNED YOU.

"They've spotted us." Banana typed like a crazed wood-pecker. "Engaging evasive maneuvers!"

The Volt Hammer was now chanting *waga waga goo-ga!* and I had to shout over it to be heard. "We're glowing purple!"

"Purple? There is no purple," said Banana.

"There is now."

"Meter reading?" he asked Crabapple.

"There's no meter, either," she hollered. The arrow had moved into the red zone and shattered.

"Incoming!" shouted Banana.

I looked up at the sky. "From where?"

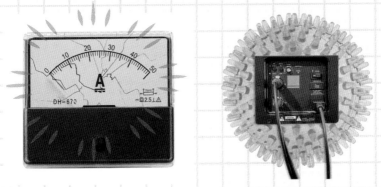

"From them!" he screamed. "They're reversing our power polarity. If it hits that Volt Hammer, we're zoinked! Cut all con-nections! Pull the power plug!"

Crabapple and I yanked on the power line that snaked its

way into his house, but it wouldn't give. Banana grabbed the throbbing Volt Hammer and flung it out of the yard, but its elastic cord made it boomerang back at him, releasing a flash of lightning that hopscotched onto every piece of **FH2** and engulfed us in a bloom of purple plasma.

In that split second between light and darkness, life and infinity, my mind was jolted into finally remembering where I had hidden my emergency stash of PEZ when I was four.

TEN SECONDS LATER

The end had not come for Crabapple and me, but buried somewhere in that smoldering mess of **FH2** was Banana. I flung computer wreckage aside while Crabapple doused the flames with a garden hose. The sound of moaning led me to a terrible sight: Banana's shirt was scorched, and his pants were torn, but his face . . . his face was a dripping mess of chunky red goo.

Someone was screaming. It was me.

DIARY 17
WHO DO YOU TRUST?

Although his face was a terrifying mishmash of red and white chunks, Banana blinked his eyes and licked his lips. "Relax, dude," he said to me, smiling. "It's Spaghetti Ready!"

I didn't know whether to kiss or hit him, so I helped him up and Crabapple rinsed him off with the hose. It may have been the first time that his *Supreme* shirt had gotten a cleaning. He immediately set about scavenging the wreckage of **FH2** and planning for **FH3**. "Next time," he vowed, "I won't mix Apple with PC."

"There won't be a next time," said Crabapple.

"Why not?" I asked.

"I've found the manual. That's what I tried to tell you when you got here."

This caught me off guard. Why wasn't she jumping up and down and screaming "Yay"? Not that she ever had.

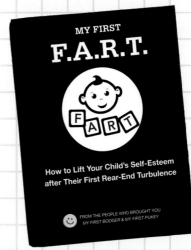

"You drowned a cannibal?" asked Banana.

"I FOUND THE MANUAL," she shouted. "You've got spaghetti in your ears." She pulled a black book out of her backpack. "Here it is."

There it was.

She passed it to me. "How'd you get it?" I asked.

"I asked my parents for it and they gave it to me. It was that simple. The deadline for my news story got moved up and I still had no evidence, so I figured, why not ask?"

I took a closer look at the book.

Crabapple continued, "They said that now that I was grown up, they didn't need it anymore."

"This isn't the **F.A.R.T.** manual," I told her.

"But you just said it was."

"I know, but it's not. This is a book on *how* to fart."

"That IS the **F.A.R.T.** manual," she insisted.

"It isn't. Do you want to know what I think?"

"No."

"I think that this is a decoy book that **F.A.R.T.** uses to fake kids out."

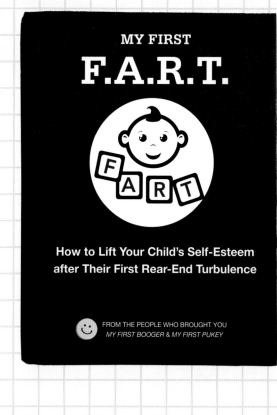

MY FIRST

F.A.R.T.

How to Lift Your Child's Self-Esteem after Their First Rear-End Turbulence

FROM THE PEOPLE WHO BROUGHT YOU
MY FIRST BOOGER & MY FIRST PUKEY

"Oh, get real," she replied. "Let's face it—there is no **F.A.R.T.** We've tried every which way to prove it."

"You want proof?" I asked. "Look what's happened to us. Look what they did to Banana."

"Popcorn, it's a miracle Banana hasn't blown himself up long before this."

"Actually, I have," said Banana as he booted up his laptop.

"And yes," continued Crabapple, "he hacked into a website, but whose? We still don't know."

"What about Apricot?" I said. "She said she found the manual."

"She *may* have found *something*, but first we have to find Apricot, don't we? Maybe she found out that there isn't a manual and she doesn't want to hurt your feelings. You know how she is."

"How do you explain Clabby?"

"Clabby? What's a Clabby?" she asked. "Where do you get this stuff? We're done. And so's my Big Story." She put the fake **F.A.R.T.** manual into her backpack and turned to leave.

"Quitter," I said after her.

She spun around and pointed her finger at me. "You take that back."

"No."

"No one has worked harder to prove that **F.A.R.T.** exists. No one."

"No one's worked harder to throw us off course, you mean. Who arranged to buy that first fake manual? You did. And when that didn't discourage us, who tried to talk us out of believing in a Brain Modem? You did. Who came up with the password to a website that blew up in our faces? You did. And now who shows up with another bogus manual that's supposed to make us give up and go home?"

"What? So now I'm working for **F.A.R.T.**? Is that it? I'll do you one better, Popcorn." She pulled on her ears. "I've got a Brain Modem implanted in my head. That's right. I admit it. BUT AT LEAST I'VE GOT A BRAIN TO PUT IT IN!"

"Fellas?" Banana raised his hand meekly.

Crabapple kept swinging. "The only reason why any of this happened is because WE BELIEVED YOU. Period."

"Fellas?" repeated Banana as he tapped the enter key on his laptop over and over. "Not for nothing, but I don't exist anymore. My blogs, my postings, my websites are gone. My passwords don't work. These guys sucked me into their website like a newbie, and then they wiped me out." He threw the laptop into the remains of **F.A.R.T. HACKER 2**. "I don't exist."

Crabapple put her hand on Banana's shoulder. "You exist. At least you're not selling real estate for the rest of your life."

I sat down next to Banana and the three of us observed a moment of silence for the fallen **FH2**. Then Banana called Crazy Davey's Computer Crunchers to haul his beloved creation away. That had to hurt.

I thought about what I had said to Crabapple. It all made perfect sense, and it was all wrong. I couldn't even look her in the eye when I said, "I take it back. I say stupid things when I get blown up. Would you like to believe me one last time?"

"Do I have to?"

"No."

"Okay," she sighed. "What's a Clabby?"

DIARY 18
STEALING MRS. PUCKOWITZ

Crabapple and I set off to see Dr. Clabby while Banana waited for Crazy Davey to haul off **FH2**. Finding Clabby's home should have been easy—I'd been there that morning—but the houses all looked alike, and when we found 26 Lover's Lane, the sign on his mailbox naming him "The World's Most Successful Author" was missing. I guess that's what threw me off.

I knocked on the door.

"Wait till you see this guy," I told her.

But we didn't see that guy. What we saw when the door opened was a nice older couple watching the Furniture Channel: "All Furniture, All the Time."

I peeked inside. Gone was Clabby's clutter—the ads, the

boxes of cookies, and the filing cabinets. The couple acted confused when I mentioned Clabby. "Well, bless my buttons," said the old lady. "We've lived here for years, and we've

Furniture in Sport

Documentary

never heard of this Clabby fellow, have we, Elmer?"

Maybe it was 62 Lover's Lane or 266 Lover's Lane that we wanted?

By now, I was used to people telling me that I was mistaken or confused, so I kept cool. "This is the place," I whispered to Crabapple. "I was here."

"Sorry to bother you folks," said Crabapple. "We'll be going now."

"Wait!" I told her. "I can prove this is Clabby's house."

I dragged her to the mailbox as the couple looked on. "Look under the mailbox."

"Why?"

"Don't be afraid. Look."

She did.

"What do you see?"

"Gum."

"Exactly."

"So?"

"I put it there this morning."

"How do I know it's your gum?"

"Because it's pot-roast-flavored gum. No one else has gum like that. Peel it off and taste it."

"Used gum? No, thanks."

"I'm telling you—these people were not living here this morning."

"Popcorn, let me guess," said Crabapple. "These people are actors hired by **F.A.R.T.** to take the place of Dr. Clabby."

"Yes! Exactly!"

Crabapple looked skyward. "Popcorn, seek help. Okay? Bye."

"Just wait here," I pleaded. "Don't move."

There was no way that **F.A.R.T.** could have gotten rid of Clabby and emptied his place without leaving some clue behind. I ran inside and spotted what I was looking for—a bird-cage hanging in the corner. Sure! That's where **F.A.R.T.** slipped up. Mrs. Puckowitz. People could ignore me, but they couldn't ignore a parrot that says, "Fart is real! Fart is real!" Ha! No one could.

I grabbed the cage and rushed to the door.

The old lady stood in my way. "You put her back. I'll call the police!"

"Go ahead, you old bat!" I cried as she whacked me with a pillow with the words **BINGO CHAMP** on it. "And tell **F.A.R.T.** that Furious Popcorn is coming for them!"

When I got outside, Crabapple was gone. She'd had enough, I guess. The Only Onlys bond between us had been broken and I was the guy who did it. I vowed to make things right again, but first, it was time to fly.

I knew that the police would be circu- lating sketches of me and Mrs. Puckowitz all over town, but Johnny Law does not use skateboards, so I had the edge. But where could I go?

DIARY 19
ASK GRANDPA—HE KNOWS

Would you like a Hot Pocket?"

That's how my grandma says "hello."

"No, thanks," I replied. "I just came to visit."

"Have one anyway. What would your parrot like?"

It hadn't taken me long to get to my grandparents' place, although skateboarding with a parrot cage is never easy. They lived in one of those old-geezer communities where everyone smiles, says hello, and then keeps talking to you. I'm not putting them down or anything. They're lonely. I was lonely myself.

After feeding Mrs. Puckowitz (who hadn't said a word since I swiped her), I downed a steak, French fries, a green-bean casserole with canned crumbly onions, and a Hot Pocket. I eat when I'm nervous.

While Grandma packed me a doggie bag, my grandfather invited me to watch *Wheel of Fortune*, something we've been doing since I was little. I loved watching Grandpa yell stuff like "chowderhead" and "numbskull" whenever the contestants were clueless.

As I settled in on the sofa—the awesome kind with cup holders—Grandpa slipped me a Mentos and whispered as he glanced at Grandma, "Don't tell the Iron Oven Mitt that I'm eating these."

"I won't, Grandpa."

"Good man."

During the commercial he took a swig of Ensure and turned to me. "It's none of my beeswax, but something's bothering you. Few people can eat a Hot Pocket without defrosting it. What's on your mind?"

I can tell my grandpa anything because no one believes him anymore. He had, to quote my father, "ventured into the unusual lately," what with writing letters to President Nixon and leaving phone messages like "Where's my hovercraft?"

On the other hand, I wouldn't count this guy out. He used

to be in some kind of law enforcement, and he still had his edge. You should see him take apart telemarketers.

I got right to the point. "Grandpa, I found a **F.A.R.T.** manual."

It got so quiet, you could hear my grandma's pacemaker in the next room.

"What's more, I know what they're planning to do, but I don't know how to stop it."

"Great googly moogly," gushed Grandma as she hurried in. "A **F.A.R.T.** manual? What on earth could that be? What an imagination our grandson has. Don't you think so, Skeeter?" That was her pet name for him.

Grandpa turned up the TV's volume, hoping to avoid the whole situation. I gently took the remote from him and muted the TV.

"Grandpa, tell me the truth. You always have."

He stared at the silent TV and said, "Forget you ever saw that book."

"But you said that it's always better to know things."

Tears welled up in his eyes.

"Skeeter," admonished Grandma, "don't do it."

He scowled at her and asked, "What can **F.A.R.T.** do to me now?"

DIARY 20
GRANDMA KNOWS TOO

My grandma stood in the kitchen doorway drying her hands on a dish towel while Grandpa told me his story: "I stumbled onto that manual as a child," he began, "just as you did, and it bugged me something fierce. My parents found out and took it back. Naturally, no one believed me and I forgot about it. That's the blessing of youth. But the years passed, I had kids of my own, and they drove me hot jiminy cracker-bats. Why, your father . . ." His voice trailed off as he relived a terrible memory. "So when that manual came back into our lives, it made things easier. You'll feel differently when you're older. I'm not saying it's right. Don't think we haven't fretted about it. . . ." He sank deeper into his chair.

"Grandpa, do you still have it? The manual?"

My grandma rested her oven mitt on my shoulder.

"The Plumbers took it back just after your father went to high school," she said. "Once a kid hits fifteen or so, nothing much works after that."

I rose and hugged her. This hadn't been easy for either of them.

I told them the rest of my story—how I had found and lost the manual, about the Brain Modem, and what had happened to the Only Onlys after they'd tried to help. "We keep collecting these clues," I said, "but they either go nowhere or they blow up in our faces."

My grandfather smiled. "Feeling sorry for yourself?"

"A little."

"Go ahead," he said. "You've earned it. These fellas you're tangling with are good. Real good! Heck, they're almost as good as . . ." Grandpa sat up and studied me with a steely gaze. "I'm going to tell you something, my boy. It may give you a leg up, or it may be a load of old guff from your crazy grandpa, but I'll only say it once and never again. Check?"

"Check," I replied. Something big was coming. My guts were churning, though it might have been that Hot Pocket.

"A long time ago I worked for a secret agency deep within our government. That's all I can say about it. Now, the opposition—or the 'bad guys,' as we called them—were always after our secrets, just like we were after theirs. So we created fake secrets to mess with their heads. Like, once we put guards around an empty warehouse and dropped hints that a secret weapon was inside. Those poor enemy spies went nuts trying to get in there, and all for nothing. Ha! I almost felt sorry for them. They looked so lost and frustrated, just like you do now." He laughed and tousled my hair.

"Grandpa, do you think that's what **F.A.R.T.** is doing to us?"

"Beats me," he replied, "but you're on someone's radar, no doubt about it. They're filling you with so many stories and humbug that pretty soon you won't know the truth from a lie and you won't even care. Heck, **F.A.R.T.** will be the least of your worries."

The old guy knew what he was talking about. I thought about how the Only Onlys had changed since tangling with

F.A.R.T. Crabapple was going to sell real estate. Banana had gotten kicked out of cyberspace. Apricot—wherever she was—had become a science whiz. And I was a has-been ViewTube star who vacuumed the house looking for spy cameras. We'd become everything our parents wanted us to be. This couldn't be an accident. There was a force at work here. Not *the* Force, just *a* force.

"Grandpa, what do I do now?"

"If I were a younger man, I'd do to them what they're doing to you."

"How?"

"Figure it out. I'm retired." Grandpa unmuted the TV just in time for a commercial to blare at him—the wrong commercial, apparently. "This guy again?" he fumed.

Naturally, the more Grandpa tried to turn the TV down, the louder it got.

Jack Hack from **Fearless Publishing** was on. He promised to

print YOUR book and make YOU rich! Which got me thinking—if I still had my parents' manual, I'd call Jack and have him reprint it for the whole world to see. After all, **F.A.R.T.** could shut down a blog or censor a video, but a book was something else. It was old tech, but powerful tech just the same. If only I could find that manual!

"Grandpa? Where would a spy hide something?"

"I never said I was a spy," he replied. He leaned in close with his Mentos breath and whispered, "Although people think I'm loopy, but that's just to fool the opposition."

"I think it's working, Grandpa."

"What was your question?"

"Where's the best place to hide something?"

"That's easy," he said. And he told me.

It *was* easy.

Then he looked at the TV and shouted, "Someday it will all become clear!"

"Someday it will all become clear," said the *Wheel of Fortune* contestant on the TV, solving the puzzle and winning a trip to a place filled with palm trees.

"It's about time, nitwit," shouted Grandpa.

Someday it will all become clear. Yes, indeed. I knew exactly where to look for my parents' manual and what I would do when I found it.

SOMEDAY IT WILL ALL BECOME CLEAR

I grabbed my doggie bag and my parrot and said my good-byes.

As I opened the door to leave, Grandpa tossed his keys to me. "It's getting dark, my boy. Take my hovercraft."

DIARY 21
A FRESH START

My first stop after leaving my grandparents was 26 Lover's Lane to return a parrot. Mrs. Puckowitz hadn't said a word since I'd stolen her, so I assumed she wasn't the real Mrs. Puckowitz at all; just another **F.A.R.T.** fake-out. I rehearsed an apology for that poor old couple who lived there now, but I never got to use it—26 Lover's Lane was abandoned. A **FOR SALE** sign hung from its mailbox, and the pot-roast-flavored gum that I had stuck under it had vanished. The realtor listed on the sign was Crabapple's mother. (Interesting, yes?)

Arriving home, I expected to see the police at my door, but all was quiet. My parents were attending their book club, or a **F.A.R.T.** meeting, but either way it gave me a chance to try

Grandpa's advice about where the manual might be:

"In a place that's already been searched, my boy. That's where you should look."

It turned out to be good advice.

Not long after, my phone started pinging:

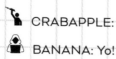

CRABAPPLE: We're outside.

BANANA: Yo!

I opened my front door and saw Crabapple and Banana stepping out of the shadows. In the light of the moon, they looked like Squid Kids again.

"I didn't think I'd see you guys for a while," I said. "Maybe never."

Sharing gum is **HAZARDOUS** to your health.

Crabapple opened her notebook and clicked her pen. "I thought we should brainstorm about **F.A.R.T.** and the Brain Modem," she said. "There's not much time."

"What brought you back?" I asked her. "What changed your mind?"

She spit out something that dinged our garden gnome.

"Gum," she replied. "Used pot-roast-flavored gum."

Holy guacamole! Crabapple had gone back to Clabby's, peeled that gum off the bottom of his mailbox, and chewed it, just like I had asked her. Apricot might be right: Bossy Boots really did like me.

"The first thing we should do," I said, "is find Apricot."

"Absopositively," said Banana, "and second, I'll build **F.A.R.T. HACKER 3**."

"Third," I added, "Crabapple should finish her Big Story about **F.A.R.T.**"

"Popcorn, I still need evidence," she said. "No evidence, no story."

I reached under my shirt and pulled out the **F.A.R.T.** manual in all its genuine glory. "Now you've got it."

Crabapple and Banana gazed upon it in awe.

"You know, Popcorn," said Crabapple, "even with this manual as evidence, I doubt my school adviser will print my story."

"Why not?" I asked.

"She's a parent, Popcorn. A parent."

"Well, I know someone who will print your story," I replied. "In fact, he'll print the whole manual. Have you guys ever heard of Jack Hack?"

Another **EXCLUSIVE** from **Fearless Publishing!**

THIS IS YOUR **LUCKY** DAY!

F.Ä.R.T.

TOP SECRET! NO KIDS ALLOWED!

"If you read only one book this year, then you're not reading enough books, dummy."

—Jack Hack
Publishe

You've heard about it. You've wondered about it. And now you've got it—the ultra-secret parents' manual that no kid was ever meant to see!

How did I get it? This Furious Popcorn kid dropped it on my desk and said, "If you're really fearless, you'll print this!" I had security throw him out. It's fun to call security on teenagers. Anyway, it looked like a joke. Come on! F.A.R.T.?

But the more I thought about it, the more I couldn't stop reading it. Some of you will believe it, and some of you won't. Hey, as long as you pay for it, I don't care!

HERE'S THE DEAL: This is the first part of the manual. Furious Popcorn tells me there's more to come. Says he doesn't trust me with the whole thing yet! Can you believe that? ME?! Honest Jack Hack?

So, is it a joke? You decide.

ABOUT THE AUTHOR

After starting as an intern at Walt Disney Studios, **PETER BAKALIAN** joined the production team for Rankin/Bass's *ThunderCats* and later earned Emmy recognition for his writing on *Curious George*. He was also nominated along with Suzanne Collins for Best Animated Screenplay by the Writers Guild of America for the Fox musical special *Santa, Baby!*, which he also produced. His work has also appeared on the BBC series *Big & Small* and Scholastic's *Clifford's Puppy Days*. *F.A.R.T.* is his first novel.

MANUAL SECTIONS

PRANKS

SCHOOL

CONTEST

HEALTH

SPY TIME

GAMES

blah!
bleh!
blah!

EAT

HOROSCOPE

WORDS

HOME

MON

Here's the first third of the F.A.R.T. manual. Can't risk putting it all in one place. More to come in the next book, I promise. Stay furious, my friends!

—Furious Popcorn

KID LIT

CYBERWA

ease place F.A.R.T. bulletins and newsletters in your manual.

PRANKS

HOW TO RUIN YOUR KIDS' FUN
PART 1: RUIN THEIR MUSIC

Your kids know what drives you insane.

That's why they do it.

For example, do you think they really like the music they listen to? Of course not. But kids play it. And they play it **LOUD**. **WHY?** Because **YOU** hate it, melonhead. So here's what you do. . . .

> **LIKE WHAT YOUR KIDS LIKE, AND THEY'LL HATE IT.**

It's easy. Buy some "bling," call yourself "Cream Cheese Daddy," and hang out with your kids when their friends visit. Will you look totally oogie like pops above? Sure, but think of those awesome gold chains you'll get to wear!

How can this guy...

What a noob!

beat this kid at video games?

HE CHEATS! And you can too! We figured it out in the

F.A.R.T. SCIENCE LAB.

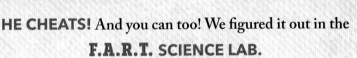

A F.A.R.T. SCIENCE LAB EXCLUSIVE ✳

We link your ordinary-looking controller directly to the hard-core gamers below.

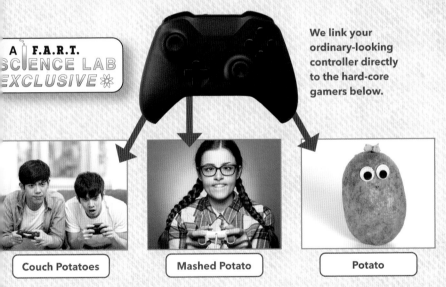

Couch Potatoes

Mashed Potato

Potato

So, when your kid challenges you to a game, he's really playing these puds. You can't lose!

AND HERE'S THE BEST PART—you don't have to pay these jokers anything. They've got nothing else to do. Nice, huh?

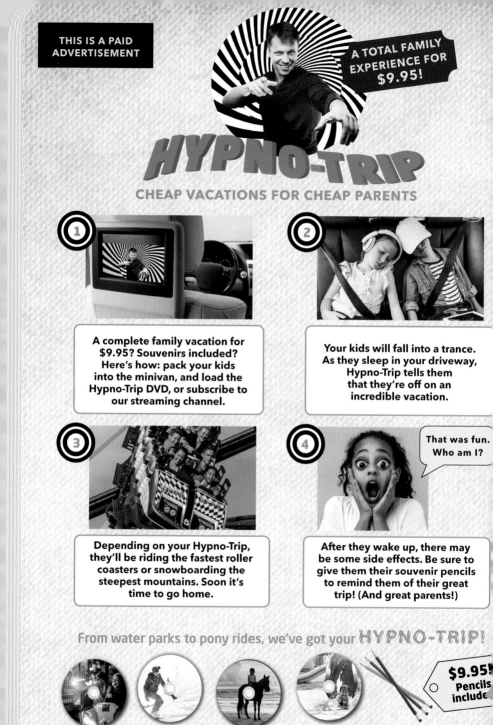

When a kid acts goofy **THE MOMENT** you snap a picture, that's **A PHOTOBOMB**.

Introducing the

PHOTOBOMB
Buster Camera

00:00:20:20

MENU ≡

BOMB!

ISO 100 1/100 F2.8

The new Bomb Buster camera looks like an ordinary camera, and that's a good thing. Photobombers never give you a warning. Why give them one?

⬅ 1. Set camera menu to "PHOTOBOMB."

2. When the camera detects a PHOTOBOMB in progress, it releases forty gallons of compressed water. Does it work? Turn the page. ➡

PRODUCT TEST
PHOTOBOMB BUSTER CAMERA

At left, we see a possible photobomb in progress. Bomb Buster analyzes his face: Is he attempting a bomb, or is he just goofy? The camera's sensors decide: **IT'S A BOMB!**

Bomb Buster's forty gallons of water zap the photobomber without spilling a drop onto his mom. We did this five times in a row with the same result. **AMAZING!**

What a great picture! No photobomb, and uh, where'd that kid go? Anyway, Bomb Buster's a winner in our book! **HIGHLY RECOMMENDED!**

★★★★★ **EXCELLENT!**

A Letter from *Lola*

here, fellow **F.A.R.T.**ees! Welcome to our
sletter. We've got new pages for your manual,
rity updates, and surprises galore. Mrs. W. sent
is month's tip (right) and the **SNEAKY CANDY**
w) is a "must-have" for the holiday season. Sweet!

ove ya! Lola

TIP OF THE MONTH:
"Never taste your kid's
ice cream."

SNEAKY CANDY
**Just sneak 'em into the
candy bowl. Your kids will
get the message.**

SECURITY *WITH STIG*

URING SECURITY CHIEF STIG PLUNGER

tten Kid Incidents (**R.K.I.**) increased in
tors 7 & 15 due to parents' carelessness with their
nuals. My 24-Hour Plumbers retrieved all missing
oks.

wedish parents blog mentioned **F.A.R.T.** by
ne. We shut them down as a routine precaution.

.R.T. research is testing **THE BRAIN MODEM**
ttom right). Early results are promising.

w manual covers will be released shortly.

STIG, OUT.

SECRET HANDSHAKE
changes this month

old   new

EXPERIMENTAL BRAIN MODEM
Project funded by your kids'
bake sales and magazine
subscriptions.

SCHOOL

Solve your kid's homework problems, even if you're a nitwit.

LET'S FACE IT, PAL— you were no genius in school, and you haven't gotten any smarter. So, when your kid asks for help with her homework, you're in **BIG** trouble.

Sure, you can hire a smart kid (right) to secretly teach you the answers, but those kids are expensive. Many of them smell funny too.
But there's hope. . . .

DO WHAT TEACHERS DO!

>T FOR STUDENT USE

MATH

CAN BE IMPOSSIBLE

TEACHER'S EDITION
Contains answers no student
will ever figure out

Get the teacher's edition of your kid's textbooks. That's how teachers know the answers, and so will you!

Yes, we here at **F.A.R.T.** will charge you lots of money for these books, but we're cheaper than that kid. We smell better too. Imagine answering the questions below as if you actually knew something:

John buys three hundred pineapples. He gives half to Mary, the other half to Chris, and the last half to Angela. How much candy corn would John have to leave under his pillow to fool the tooth fairy into leaving him enough money to buy three hundred pineapples?

A grocery bag measures 2 by 3 by 4 inches. What's in the bag?

Have your class draw a perfect square. Is it a perfect square? If so, how perfect? Says who? (Teacher's note: focus on one kid, and ask her, "How perfect?" again and again until the student gives up. A question like this keeps the smarter kids in line.)

You tell a friend who is coming to visit that your house number is 2x1/3+360°. What will your friend need to solve this problem?

a) A lawyer to get her out of jail for breaking into the wrong house.
b) A better friend than you who won't mess with her.
c) A rocket ship to Mars, where houses have addresses like this.

Contact your local F.A.R.T. representative.
Order your teacher's edition today!

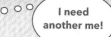

YOU DON'T HAVE TO TAKE . . . .

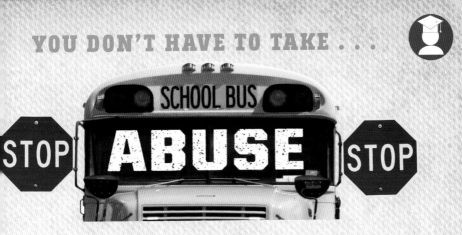

SCHOOL BUS ABUSE

STOP **STOP**

We've all been there. You're at a red light when a school bus pulls up alongside you. You've got to stop. It's the law. Fine. Great. But where is "the law" when this happens?

...re is no excuse for this.

And let's not forget the flying lunches!

Does **F.A.R.T.** have a solution? Of course we do. It's drastic and expensive, but how much school bus abuse can you take?

Dig out your wallet, and turn the page!

PROPERTY OF F.A.R.T. • DO NOT DUPLICATE

INTRODUCING . . .

THE BUS BUSTER GT

FEATURES:

- **BUILT-IN ATOMIC REACTOR** means no more gas stops.
- **SPLAT-PROOF GLASS.**
- **FOUR HUNDRED CUP HOLDERS. FOUR HUNDRED!**
- **PARK WHERE YOU WANT.** Who's going to stop you?

NO MORE:

- **SCHOOL BUS HOOLIGANS.**
- **DISCOURTEOUS DRIVERS.**
- **DAWDLING PEDESTRIANS.**

FIRE-DEPARTMENT-CERTIFIED WATER CANNONS.*

Next month's auto review: child ejector seats—which brand is best

*Listen, about those water cannons: you really shouldn't use them on school buses, and certainly not when someone's recording it on one of those pesky smartphones.

ACE the Parent-Teacher Conference

Worried about your parent-teacher conference? You should be. If they bounce your kid out of school, he'll be yours **ALL DAY**. Here's **ACTUAL RECORDING** of one so you know what to expect.

TEACHER: Hello, and thanks for coming. Have a seat.

PARENTS: Ouch! Wow, these chairs are uncomfortable.

TEACHER: Yeah, the kids sit on those. Keeps 'em awake.

PARENTS: So, about our son, do you think he has potential?

TEACHER: Who knows? He's a kid. They're all kids.

PARENTS: But, we thought . . .

TEACHER: Just look at his artwork. He drew a picture of a guy with three noses. If he sneezes, his ears will explode. What's up with that? And this is the best of the bunch!

PARENTS: How about math? Our son seems to get the right answers.

TEACHER: By accident, believe me. To tell you the truth, if I didn't have the answer book, I'd be lost.

PARENTS: What do you think about his writing? Is he doing well?

TEACHER: You tell me. The stuff they hand in is so sloppy, no one can read it!

PARENTS: Then how do you grade the papers?

TEACHER: I don't. My dog does. He sniffs out the As, the Bs, you get the idea?

PARENTS: Are you serious?

TEACHER: Hey, my dog WENT to this school!

PARENTS: What if you gave extra homework? Maybe it would help.

TEACHER: Nah. We give homework to keep kids off the streets at night.

PARENTS: So homework is . . . useless?

TEACHER: (Giggles.) Oh my, yes. Well, I'd say we're done here, but you can't leave yet.

PARENTS: Why not?

TEACHER: A long meeting makes your kids think that they're in trouble. That's always good. How about a game of cards?

END OF RECORDING.

See? The teacher is on **YOUR** side. Just let her win at poker.

SUBSTITUTE TEACHER:

THE WORLD'S
WORST
JOB

A recent study confirms that substitute teaching is even worse than these jobs:

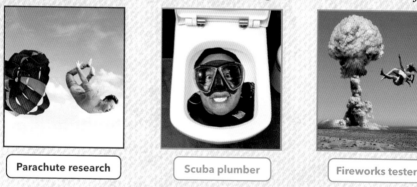

Parachute research **Scuba plumber** **Fireworks tester**

Are you a substitute teacher? (Too bad.) Here are

THE SIX BIG LIES KIDS TELL SUBSTITUTE TEACHERS:

1. We're substitute students.
2. Please call on someone else. I'm the air marshal for this flight.
3. This isn't math class. It's French class. You first, Pierre.
4. The principal's office called. They said, "You're fired."
5. We're Santa's helpers. Be nice, or the big guy's bringing you nothing.
6. It's your turn to pay the pizza delivery guy.

CONTEST
WE HAVE A WINNER!

st month we asked:

hat's your secret to keeping your kid's room neat and clean?

R WINNER: Ms. Ida Haddit, inventor and mom.

COULDN'T TAKE IT ANYMORE! Each
rning I would clean my kid's room, only to have it
ssed up by the end of the day.
at's why I created **ROOM GLUE!**
rong enough to glue together an exploded asteroid,
om Glue literally sticks everything in your kid's
m to everything else. Nothing gets out of place
ause it can't go anyplace."

RNED

INTO
THIS.
FOREVER.

nce again, **F.A.R.T.** congratulates Ms. Haddit for her prize-winning invention.
e bet you're wondering if Room Glue can be used to glue kids to their chairs so
ey'll do their homework. We're not saying you should, but what an interesting idea!
HANK YOU ALL FOR ENTERING OUR CONTEST, AND BETTER LUCK
EXT TIME!

HEALTH

FROM ONE PARENT TO ANOTHER:
YOUR KID STINKS!

"Get it?"

Does the smell of your kid trigger your airbag?
Does your dog try to bury him in the backyard?
Face it—your kid's a dirt ball.

Here are some FAILS.

PUT THEM THROUGH A CAR WASH

FAIL

BUNGEE
INTO A
WASHING
MACHINE.

STUPID FAIL

BUY A COMBO DISH-
AND-KID-WASHER.*

ANOTHER FAIL!

*SORRY, KID-WASHERS
NO LONGER SOLD.
TOO MANY BROKEN DISHES.

The answer:
BATH BOMBS!

hat will your kids think when you serve up water balloons? They'll think
u're one of those "new" kind of parents—the sensitive type who wants
em to have fun and be their friend. **HA!** They won't even realize that
ey're taking a bath. And you? You're laughing at them. Yes, laughing!
A! HA! HA! Just like that.

Don't stand around and watch.

WASH

The blue balloons are filled
with **TSUMANI-6 CLEANER**—
strong enough to clean an entire
city! Wow!

RINSE

The green balloons are filled with
RINSE AID for a sneaky clean!

WAX

Next comes the wax for a long-
lasting shine. Always use Bath
Bombs brand **TEEN WAX** for
quality results!

REPEAT

Much better.

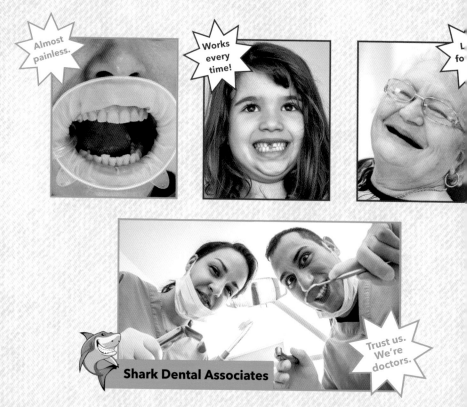

YOU NEED A REPORT CARD VACCINE!

Hello. I'm a picture of a doctor. Every day parents go into terrible shock after seeing their kids' report card. Don't let it happen to you. Get our new vaccine: **WORLD'S WORST REPORT CARD.** You'll be une to whatever your kid brings home. Please follow irections below.

PLEASE BE SEATED. • READ SLOWLY. • BREATHE DEEPLY. • YOU MAY BEGIN.

East Bumblenuts Regional School
Home of the Nutty Squirrels
Student Progress Report

Student: <u>Rick O'Shea</u> **Homeroom Teacher**: <u>Robin Banks</u> **Grade**: <u>7</u>

SUBJECT	GRADE	OVERALL COMMENT	SPECIAL NOTES
Science	F	Student believes that the Moon is taken down and cleaned during the day.	208, 712
Math	F	When performing long division, feels sorry for remainders, and refuses to round them off.	220, 760
cial Studies	F	Claims World War II was between Earth and Krypton.	356, 756
nguage Arts	F	Wants extra credit for eating alphabet soup.	152, 300, 328
Art	F	Heather is enormously talented. Too bad your kid isn't Heather.	228, 412
Computer	F	Sold entire school building on a real estate website. Teachers included.	240, 416
Health/PE	F	Student living inside gym locker. Plays music too loud. Neighbors complaining.	204

INDEX TO REPORT CARD SPECIAL NOTES

Tells first graders that his locker is the elevator to Santa's workshop. Charges $1 per ride.
Enjoys working alone, which is good, because she's totally annoying.
Two issues: this student is forgetful and . . . something else.

152	Does not proofread compleated assignments.
204	Fails to bring supplies to school. Underwear counts as "supplies."
208	Failure to make up work.
212	Failure to work makeup. Eyeliner smeared. Lipstick simply awful.
220	Assignments are complete, but never correct . . . which means they're useless.
228	Hair parted on wrong side.
232	Your child may be happier in a different solar system.
240	Uses whipped cream for hair gel. Flies living behind ears.
244	Spread a nasty rumor about the "P" in PSAT.
300	Tongue surfs in water fountain. Claims to be practicing for the Olympics.
328	Makes friends easily. Enemies disappear mysteriously after recess.
340	Insists there is a Boys for Snots campaign and he's just helping out.
356	Never prepared. When called on in class, tells teacher: "Whatever they're paying you, I'll double it!"
364	Always willing to help a classmate if the price is right.
412	Grades dropped drastically as the semester went on. Does this kid still go here?
416	Taunts guidance counselor with "Look how your career turned out!" remarks.
424	Poor math skills. Owes principal $10. Claims it's $5.
504	Burping the Pledge of Allegiance does not count.
712	Leaves his Big Wheel in principal's parking space.
748	Every time the school bell rings, student yells: "Hey, ma, the waffles are ready!"
756	Uses math flash cards to run poker games during recess.
760	Sent pizza delivery guys to pose as his parents for parent-teacher conference. Pizza was cold. Toppings were not fresh.

STOP! You have just read the world's worst report card. Take a breath. Relax. Remember, this is not your kid's report card. It is a vaccine. NEXT MONTH: *telltale signs that your kid's science project is about to EXPLODE.*

YOU CAN'T HANDLE GRANNY CANDY, AND NEITHER CAN YOUR KID.

Grannies are tough. Tougher than you. That's how they got to be that o
And the sweets they eat are the Terminators of the candy world. So wh
Grandma Gravyboat serves these up, you know enough to say, "No, thanks.

But then this happens:

**Granny offers candy to
your kid. You warn her
that she won't like it.
You say *NO!***

**Your kid thinks you are
an idiot. Of course she'll
like it! She begs. You
believe her.**

**Kid hates the candy a
spits it in your hand. Y
knew it was going to
happen. You *ARE* an id**

LET'S GET SMARTER ABOUT THIS. READ ON.

KNOW your GRANNY CANDY!

BLACK LICORICE: The Cheapo Candy Company must have wondered: Can we make candy out of tires? They could, and they did.

LOOGY METER

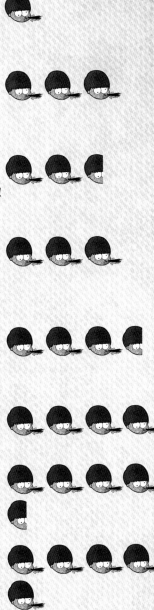

CANDY CORN: Imagine teeth that have never been brushed. Yum! These sugar bombs have fouled Halloween bags for years.

HARD CANDY: No one really knows who makes them, where you buy them, how old they are, or what's in them. But Granny's always got 'em!

RIBBON CANDY: Breaks into a jillion pieces on your face with one bite. Nice.

CHOCOLATE-COVERED RAISINS:
Looks like something a rabbit left behind. Sold in movie theaters, where you can't buy much else. And, thankfully, you can't see them in the dark.

BOXED CANDY: Chocolate-covered who-knows-what? You always think that the next one will be better. It never is.

FRUIT CAKE: Gummy bears trapped inside a huge hockey puck. Enough said.

CHOCOLATE-COVERED CHERRIES:
It's a nice milk chocolate ball filled with guts. Kids think: I like chocolate. I like cherries. I'll like this. **NO. THEY. WON'T.**

F.A.R.T. BULLETIN

YOUR MANUAL'S CHANCE OF SELF-DESTRUCT:

Here's the last section for now. More to come. Don't worry. It gets even worse! Watch for it! Stay furiou my friends!

—Furious Popcor

Where is your manual, Mr. & Mrs. Parents?

Your manual, number <u>**3278**</u>, may be missing.

Find it.

Your manual's chance of self-destruct is now **MODERATE**.

If you have found your manual, return the post card below.

BUSINESS REPLY MAIL
FIRST-CLASS MAIL PERMIT NO. 452 ANY CITY NY

NO POSTAGE
NECESSARY
IF MAILED
IN THE
UNITED STATES

24-HOUR PLUMBERS
P. O. BOX 4711
SEPTIC, NEW JERSEY 00000